It takes three minutes to choke to death . . .

"I guess it must seem longer to the one doing the choking."

While the German was talking, Specs leaned over from his saddle and hooked the noose over my head and snugged what knot there was up under my left ear.

I kept my seat as long as I could, my thigh muscles tighter than they'd ever been, but the saddle slid smoothly between them and the stirrups hung up on my cramped toes only long enough for Chink on the ground and Specs on horseback to pull them loose. My heels grazed the chestnut's rump. And then there was just air under me and black sky above with stars punched in it . . .

THE STRANGLERS

"A doggone good Western . . . A rapid-fire plot with enough action and gunfire for a couple of books."

—*The Roundup*

THE STRANGLERS

Loren D. Estleman

JOVE BOOKS, NEW YORK

THE STRANGLERS

A Jove Book / published by arrangement with the author

PRINTING HISTORY
Previously published by Ballantine Books
Jove edition / September 1999

The Penguin Putnam Inc. World Wide Web site address is
http://www.penguinputnam.com

ISBN: 0-515-12570-9

A JOVE BOOK®
Jove Books are published by The Berkley Publishing Group,
a division of Penguin Putnam Inc.,
375 Hudson Street, New York, New York 10014.
JOVE and the "J" design
are trademarks belonging to Penguin Putnam Inc.

PRINTED IN THE UNITED STATES OF AMERICA

10 9 8 7 6 5 4 3 2 1

To Frank Ames

THE
STRANGLERS

ONE

You hear some grotesque things about what happens to a man when he's hanged; how his face turns black and his neck stretches to three feet and he soils himself, and it's all true, except you never hear about the smell.

The Indian detected it almost as early as the horses did and turned in that direction in that way they have, as if his piebald were just four extra limbs and did what he did the instant he decided to do it. We had been following the banks of a tributary of the Missouri that was dry so many months out of the year no one had bothered to give it a name, and now he swung west up a grassy slope to an aspen cluster on the crest. I signaled the others to follow and took the rear. I didn't trust the Indian; if there was something waiting up top I wanted to know about it in time to throw some lead, if it was the last lead I threw.

I was riding a sorrel gelding that year, bought at auction from the estate of a rancher who'd bred mounts for the cavalry at Fort Abraham Lincoln, and it caught wind of something ten yards up it didn't take to and tried to rear, but I drew my Deane-Adams and laid the butt along the bone behind its right ear and after that it behaved. Two more yards and I almost reared myself. You catch winds

like that on the wrong side of an outhouse on hot days when
there's been slaughtering in the vicinity. But there were no
ranches or homesteads for fifty miles, and anyway I knew
the stench. I went up there.

They hadn't bothered to do any climbing, just slung two
fairly new ropes over a limb twelve feet up and tied one
end around the trunk and the other around their customers'
throats and walked their horses out from under them, because their necks weren't broken. The pair hung as motionless as a tintype, their hands tied behind their backs and
the beginnings of bloat straining their belts and the tops of
their boots. While the five of us were watching, a big slick
blue magpie fluttered down from a high branch and perched
upside down on the head of one of them and deftly plucked
out his remaining eye. The kid we were using as guide
made a strangling sound in his throat and fired his Colt
twice at the bird, hitting it the second time in a cloud of
feathers as it took flight. Then he dismounted to be sick
behind the tree.

The Indian spat a glittering brown stream of tobacco and
said, "Hell, I'd heave too, I couldn't shoot no better'n
that."

Dad Miller told him to shut up.

The Indian threw him one of his flat black looks, but in
the end obeyed. Miller was half a foot shorter and at fifty-
two had almost thirty years on him, but the old man's
braided brown body was hard and his large broken-
knuckled fists were fast and everyone who knew him knew
it. He had been deputy U.S. marshal for nine years and had
twice turned down the offer of a presidential appointment
to marshal because it meant desk duty. Judge Harlan A.
Blackthorne, who appointed the deputies in Montana Territory, was fond of saying that a Miller roundhouse right
and a battered but breathing prisoner in the dock was worth

ten Page Murdock corpses with bullets in their backs. I'm Murdock: But good boxers make poor gun handlers, and since the country we deputies rode in those days was short on referees and long on ammunition I was running this particular show.

"Cut them down and let's see what's in their pockets," I said to the Indian.

He kneed his horse forward lazily, hiding his eagerness, and started sawing away with the short, wide blade he carried in a sheath behind his neck. His right name was Virgil Blue Water, but I had never heard anyone call him by it. He dressed like a white man, his taste running to gaudy hand-tooled boots and hats with low crowns and curled brims, but his hawk nose and narrow-lidded eyes without lashes in a round face the color of old blood said what counted. He could track a flame by its heat and a man by his shadow, and if I had half what he had and didn't need him, he'd have been on the other end of a rope like the one he was cutting years ago.

The first rope parted with a dull twang and the body thudded to the ground, followed a moment later by the other. The Indian swung out of his saddle and got to work. A few fat flies rode the stinking air, but it was too early in the season for the first hatch. The Indian ignored them crawling on his face as he probed the dead men's pockets, whistling inaccurately through his teeth.

The kid appeared from behind the tree. He rocked a little on his two-inch bootheels and his face had a bluish tinge, but I could see he was going to stick. He was maybe twenty, long and loose, with coppery down on his upper lip and his gun in an army holster turned so that the butt snugged up against his right kidney. We'd borrowed him from his father, a rancher near Painted Rock who said the boy would just be in the way during roundup anyway be-

cause he spent most of his time fishing and hunting the
north country when he should have been learning the cattle
business.

The fifth man in our crew was the killer.

You need him in every posse, the man whose brain goes
dead at the moment of decision and lets his reflexes think
for him. I've held that position once or twice, but never
fulfilled its requirements to Charley Rudabaugh's degree.
Tall, brown-eyed and soft-looking, he wore his auburn hair
over his collar mountain-fashion and a short dark beard
with gray in it, but he wasn't thirty. He carried a Schofield
high on his right hip and, I knew, a Forehand & Wadsworth
pocket gun concealed somewhere else. He wasn't fast with
either of them, but I'd seen him face faster men and he was
still here and they weren't. The difference was that when
they went for their holsters they were thinking about the
people watching and what they might tell the law and
would their gun misfire, and he wasn't thinking about anything but killing them. I don't know what he thought about
the rest of the time. Sitting his big roan there in the shade
of that tree, watching the Indian searching the two hanged
men, he looked bored and stupid. It was a look a lot of
men had taken with them to their rewards.

The Indian rose. I asked him what he got.

"Nothing with a name on it. Just this here." He held out
a soggy tobacco pouch and a handful of stained cigarette
papers.

"Where's the poke you took off one of them?"

Something moved under the skin of his face. He was still
gripping the knife he'd used to cut the ropes and slash open
the dead men's stubborn pockets. But he saw my hand resting on my thigh near the Deane-Adams and reached two
fingers inside his breast pocket and drew out a soft leather
pouch larger than the one holding tobacco. I took it and

opened it. Eleven silver dollars clanked around inside. "The Judge'll hold it for the survivors," I said, stuffing it in a saddlebag. "Supposing none of 'em shows?"

"Then they're yours. If you want to bother to put in a claim for eleven dollars."

"I cut up a man once for five dollars he owed me."

"Did he know he owed it?"

We watched each other. Dad Miller said, "Anybody know them two? Kid?"

The kid shook his head quickly. He hadn't glanced at the dead men since shooting the magpie. I said, "Look at them."

His eyes went to me, hurt, then, slowly, to the corpses lying face up on the ground. His throat muscles worked. He looked away. "No. They're strangers."

Dad said, "They ain't your ordinary drifters. Them custom boots come dear this far north. Wonder they still have them. I'd be tempted myself if their feet wasn't so damn big."

They weren't that big, but Dad was a one-time cowboy like me and proud of his size sixes.

"Nor railroad men neither," put in the Indian. "They got riding calluses."

Charley Rudabaugh said nothing. I gathered my reins.

"We'll float a reader when we get back to Helena. Mount up. We've got two hours' tracking light."

"Ain't we going to bury them?" asked the kid.

"You helped load the packs this morning," I said. "You see anything that looked like a shovel?"

"We could scratch a hole with our knives."

"*Your* knife, maybe." The Indian was putting his away. I said, "Sugar Jim's got two days on us. There'll be lots more to bury if we don't catch up soon."

"Well, can't we at least say some words over them?"

"You know any?"

"Pa makes me tote this." He produced a pocket Bible with a thumb-smeared pebbled black cover. I shrugged. He approached the bodies and leafed through the tissue pages. We took off our hats, all except the Indian, who watched with a leg hitched over his saddle horn, the tobacco bulge working in his cheek. The kid's voice was drawn thin in the open air:

" 'The hope of the righteous shall be gladness: but the expectation of the wicked shall perish. . . .'

" 'The righteousness of the upright shall deliver them: but transgressors shall be taken in their own naughtiness. . . .'

" 'Righteousness keepeth him that is upright in the way: but wickedness overthroweth the sinner. . . .'

" 'The light of the righteous rejoiceth: but the lamp of the wicked shall be put out.' "

He closed the book and turned to straddle his black. I put my hat back on, reflecting. Good Christians always seem to wind up quoting from the Old Testament, for some reason.

Sugar Jim Creel had shot and killed a government surveyor near Great Falls and fled east into the tablelands, where the one-man war of robbery and bloodletting he had waged against the government since he was sixteen had the support of cattlemen and homesteaders fed up alternately with the snubbing of and interference in their interests in Washington City. We had been the best part of a week prying information out of those close-mouthed old Indian fighters and hardscrabble farmers, but the consensus was that Creel and his partners were now too hot to risk harboring and were on their way to sanctuary in Canada. He was described as a fine-boned blond of eighteen with silver on his tongue and all the charm of a West Point lieutenant, hence his nickname. He had killed nine men that we knew of.

It was early spring, that time when the breakup in the uneven blue chalk line of the Rockies to the west was swelling even that nothing waterway we were following to a yammering torrent with gray ice shards and shattered beaver dams bobbing in the rush. The air had a snap to it, the vapor of our spent breath at sundown was as thick as milk, and in the morning we had to use our gun butts to knock loose the ice masks that formed on the horses' faces as they slept. But from midmorning to late afternoon, breathing the heady smell of fresh new grass on the medium-cool wind from the southwest was like drinking strong wine.

The sky was going maroon when the Indian dismounted to study last year's snow-flattened grass with the short green shoots showing beneath. We had come upon an old camp shortly after dawn and since then had been following the trail of four unshod horses across the rolling country-side. One set of tracks would belong to a pack animal. The Indian circled on foot for thirty yards, eyes down, then caught my attention and pointed his chin east.

"Canada's north," I reminded him.

The kid said, "They got to cross the river to get there, and this time of year the only safe ford's in that direction."

"How do you know those tracks don't belong to Indian ponies?" I asked the Indian. "There's still some Shosbone up here, and a couple of dozen Nez Percé."

"They don't ride abreast. They favor hiding how many they got with them by going single file. That was a white man's camp this morning, and anyway Sugar Jim leans to barefoot mounts to throw off trackers. Most trackers, any-how."

"What makes you such an expert on how he thinks?"

"Him and me pulled a cork or two."

I said, "You didn't tell me that going in."

"You didn't ask."

"What kind of start you figure they got on us now?" asked Dad.

The Indian spat. "Two days."

Dad said, "I'm thinking these here tracks ain't more'n a day old."

"Topsoil here holds a mark longer than most." The Indian stepped into leather. They'd had this same argument about the abandoned camp.

We cold-camped on a ridge with a thirty-degree runoff and a stand of spruce at our backs, rubbing down the horses with handfuls of grass and pulling at squares of stiff salt pork with our teeth. Dad Miller drew first watch. I left the others unrolling their blankets and walked the first few yards with him through the mottled darkness, frosted grass crunching under our boots.

"Keep alive," I told him.

He nodded once, feathery vapor fluttering at his nostrils. "The Indian?"

"You know that feeling you get when you've wounded a bear and gone after him into the bushes and you're not sure any more who's hunting who?"

"Yeah," he said, and walked the rest of the way to his post carrying his Winchester.

Back in camp I scraped together a bed of dead grass near Charley Rudabaugh and spread my blanket on top of it. Rudabaugh was sitting cross-legged on his blanket, cleaning his Schofield by moonlight with a willow twig and an oily rag. The other two members of the posse were already wrapped in wool and motionless on the other side of him.

"Anything happens," I said low, "kill the Indian."

He continued wiping and cleaning and gave no sign of

having heard. But his ears were as sharp as his reflexes. I rolled in and dropped asleep the way you do after fourteen hours pounding a saddle. I hadn't thought about the lynching since we'd left the aspens.

TWO

They hit us half an hour shy of midnight.

I don't know what I heard that brought me awake, or if I heard anything at all. I rolled out as if I'd been burned, toward the open away from Rudabaugh by instinct, just as the guns opened up, their bullets chewing my blanket where I'd been and throwing dirt pattering against my back. My Deane-Adams was out and I fired twice at the fading phosphorescence of a powder flare. Someone made a coughing grunt, but by then there were more shattering reports all around me and I couldn't place it. The moon silhouetted a man pointing a gun at me and I shot at him. He dropped away, but I couldn't tell if I'd hit him or he was just getting out of the firing line. There was another shot close by, and something that might have been the beat of hoofs going away, and then there was nothing.

In the straining silence I imagined I could hear powder smoke skidding along the ground. Then a screech owl somewhere cut loose with one of those shuddering shrieks that go straight up your spine. Somehow they always know when it's over. I got my legs under me in a tight crouch, gripping the five-shot.

"Don't shoot!"

At first I thought whoever it was was talking to me. I swiveled toward the voice, tightening on the trigger.

"Give me one good reason why I shouldn't."

The second voice—breathless, quaking—I recognized. I spoke the kid's name.

There was a pause, then: "That you, Mr. Murdock?"

I said it was. "What you got?"

"Can't see good enough to tell. Just good enough to blow his brains out if he so much as twitches."

"I ain't twitching," said the owner of the first voice.

I went for the lantern and stumbled over something big on the ground. The something groaned.

"Rudabaugh?" I said.

"Yeah." His normally soft tenor had a guttural rasp.

"Hurt bad?"

"Ain't never been hurt good."

"Hang on." I found the lantern finally, struck a match, and as the flame took hold of the wick, butter-colored light found the killer stretched out on his back to the left of his tangled blanket with his hands clasped over his abdomen. I saw the dark stain between his fingers. His Schofield was on the ground nearby and there was a large unmoving colorless lump at his feet. When I raised the lantern a dead man lay in its light. He was about twenty-five, with a lank moustache and a reddish stubble and blood glittering on his shirt. I didn't know him from Eddie Foy.

I knelt and parted Rudabaugh's hands gently to get a look at the wound and then took off my kerchief and stuffed it inside to slow the flow. He caught his breath. "Sorry," I said.

"Don't reckon I'll be feeling it much longer anyways."

I didn't say anything to that. You don't argue with a right man.

He grinned then, the white line of his teeth showing

crooked in his dark beard. "So this here's what I been handing out all these years," he said. "I'll be damned."

"More than likely." I told him to hang on again and picked up the lantern and went over to where the kid was standing with his Colt in his hand over a boy on his back on the ground with his hands resting high on his breast. Hatless, he had a thick shock of straw-colored hair and a delicate-looking face with a trace of baby fat and golden down like spun sugar on his cheeks. He didn't appear to be hurt. His eyes were pale under the lantern, but if the reader I was carrying in a pocket was reliable they were blue by daylight. The worn holster he had strapped on his left hip was empty.

"Evening, Sugar Jim," I said.

He made no answer. His eyes flicked my way momentarily, but for the most part they remained on the kid with the gun. The kid was bareheaded too, and his nose was bleeding into his puppy moustache.

"I was up taking a leak when the fracas started," he told me, without looking away from the youth on the ground. "I run back, and this'n pointed a gun at me, but I knocked it out of his hand and he slugged me. I pushed him and he fell over something. I got the drop on him then."

I covered him while the kid got my special set of manacles from my saddlebags and we locked the captive's hands behind his back and jerked him to his feet and prodded him into the middle of camp. There the kid hooked an ankle around one of Sugar Jim's and shoved him so that he fell on his face a rifle's length from Charley Rudabaugh. The kid picked up Rudabaugh's gun. I took the lantern and went looking for Dad Miller.

I found him at his post, slumped against the base of a tree. His throat was cut from corner to corner. His revolver was still in its holster and his Winchester hadn't been fired.

He'd finally found a job that his fists weren't up to. I checked on the horses. They were skittish but in good condition. One was missing, the Indian's piebald. I went back to camp.

Sugar Jim wasn't talking, but Rudabaugh still was, and with the kid's help we worked it out. While the camp was asleep the Indian had sneaked away, jumped Dad from behind, and opened his throat before he could sing out. Then he walked his horse beyond earshot of the rest of us and mounted and rode out to fetch Sugar Jim and his partners, who were much closer than even Dad had believed. I'd known the Indian was quiet but I hadn't thought he was quiet enough to beat Rudabaugh's hearing, which might explain why I slept a little more soundly than usual that night. Anyway, they came back and jumped us. Upon awakening, Rudabaugh lost a split second looking for the Indian in his bedroll, so that he fired at the same time as his assailant instead of ahead of him, killing him but getting gutshot in the process. Meanwhile I was shooting it out with the others, who had then retreated from the unexpected resistance. Walking around later with the lantern, the kid and I found some random blood spots on the grass leading away. I had at least nicked one of them. I hoped it was the Indian.

I got the whiskey flask from my saddlebags, uncorked it, and handed it to Rudabaugh, whom we had made as comfortable as possible by placing his saddle behind his head and covering him with our blankets.

The kid said, "You're not supposed to give them nothing when they're gutshot."

Rudabaugh looked at him pityingly, then tipped up the flask. Some of the red-tinted liquid spilled over his beard. He had stopped talking by now and the container required both hands to hold it up. His complexion in the lantern light was taking on that beautiful white translucence, streaked scarlet at the cheeks, that consumptives get in their last hours. He had been bleeding into his belly for some time and the external wound itself had stopped leaking. At intervals he would hawk and spit, peppering the ground with crimson.

The scant information we had gotten from the settlers in Creel country said the young killer was traveling with a cousin close to his own age named Harvey Byrd and an older man who went by Melrose. We figured Melrose was the dead man at Rudabaugh's feet. Sugar Jim didn't open his mouth to confirm or deny it.

The kid and I divided the rest of the night, spelling each other to watch Sugar Jim and look to Rudabaugh while one slept. Just before first light the kid woke me, and it was there in his silence.

"Rudabaugh?" I said.

"One minute I was talking to him, and the next I was talking to myself."

There was a quiet about him dead that went deeper than the kind he had kept when he was breathing. We manacled our prisoner's arms around the trunk of a sixty-foot pine and scouted up rocks from the river to cover Rudabaugh and Dad Miller and Melrose. We found Sugar Jim's revolver in a clump of grass and kept that for evidence and sank Dad's weapons and Rudabaugh's Schofield in the river. When you're traveling you try not to load yourself down with unnecessary iron. Dawn was sending steel shafts into the black sky when the kid finished reading from Solomon again and we got horsed, chewing salt pork. It was getting to be a good week for the wolves and magpies.

"Which way?" asked the kid.

"Helena. We got what we came for."

"What about the Indian and Byrd?"

"If they're smart they're still moving. If not we'll reel them in in a few weeks. The Judge doesn't take to having his deputies killed."

"You act like you don't care one way or the other," he said.

"You try not to make a lot of friends in this business."

Sugar Jim rode Rudabaugh's roan with his wrists chained over the saddle horn. Whatever he had ridden in on had either galloped off when the shooting started or fled with his partners. We had discarded what supplies we didn't need now that we were only three, and split up what was left between our packhorse and Dad's mount for speed. At first our captive was sullen and silent, but as the sun climbed and drew steam from the thawing grass he started humming an old drover's tune I recognized. He kept it up on and off throughout the day until the kid shouted at him to be quiet. That night we kindled our first fire in days. Sugar Jim tried to strike up a conversation over coffee, but when it didn't work he sat back with his tin cup and fell to humming again between sips. He had an open face and lively eyes and no more conscience than a wild dog. I knew his type well enough to chain him to whatever was handy and take turns watching him through the long nights.

In Great Falls I wired Judge Blackthorne a brief report, got an even briefer confirmation in that shorthand he had invented to save the government money, and borrowed a pair of sheriff's deputies to see us the rest of the way to the territorial capital. One was a sour old professional Dad's age who had fought Comanches as a Texas Ranger. The other was no older than the kid and treated the prisoner like foreign royalty because he'd read a dime novel about Sugar Jim written by a New York journalist who got all his research out of the St. Louis papers. I looked forward to getting shed of both.

Near the kid's father's ranch I shook his hand and told him to look me up if he ever felt like wearing a star.

"Not me," he said. "Believe I'll stick to cattle from here on."

He was smarter than I'd thought.

Helena didn't fit me right for a place to live anymore, which is one reason I was hardly ever there. Placer gold deposits east of the Missouri and lead and silver digs to the southwest had turned it in a few years from the rough-mannered mining town I had discovered on my first visit to the richest city per capita in the country, full of millionaires and saloons with shining cuspidors and big funny houses with more peaks and turrets than all the castles on the Rhine. Churches were going up and there was talk of a school, and pretty soon the citizens would be dressing their law in uniforms and round caps with stiff shiny black visors and there wouldn't be any welcome left for unpolished types like me who carried their badges in their pockets. All we did was remind them what things were like before we made the territory safe for the folks that didn't want us.

For the time being, though, the edges were still sharp enough for them to want us between.

Shots rang off the stone and brick buildings on Main Street just as we hit the hardpack. The horses shied, snorting, the young deputy's bay arching its back and coming down on stiff legs, almost unseating its rider, then trying again. He choked up on the reins and turned the animal in on itself. It wheeled clear around, shook its mane, and stopped. He was a better man with a horse than I would have given him credit for. By that time we all had our guns out, but all the shooting was going on at the far end of the street, and not at us.

A tall square box of a wagon was stopped there cross-wise, painted a peeling yellow with the legend COL. A HOOKSTRATTON'S FRONTIER EXTRAVAGANZA & MEDICINAL DEMONSTRATION skirling in foot-high gilt letters across the side and the more sober message AARON HOOKSTRATTON, LT. COL. RET'D., LATE ARMY OF THE REP. OF MEXICO neatly blocked underneath. A short fat man with white side-whiskers and tobacco-stained handlebars that tickled his ears stood on a platform in back, wearing dusty striped pants, a black hat like Mormons wear with a high rounded crown and a flat brim, and a buckskin jacket of a decidedly eastern cut for all the twelve-inch fringe hanging from the sleeves and down the front. Just behind him and towering over him loomed an Indian in bleached eagle feathers and a red blanket that needed washing. The wagon was hitched to a gray and a black, and since that seemed hardly enough to haul that crew plus the wagon, I assumed that at least two of the horses tethered to the rail nearby belonged to the outfit. I was pretty sure the moth-eaten buffalo tied there did. It was going white and slatsided, but the pale old horn scars along its ribs told of an interesting past.

The man doing the shooting was about my height, not tall but not short either, very thin, clean-shaven, and wore black from his kerchief to his gleaming knee-high boots. His hat, buff-colored, Texas-wide, had never held a horse's fill of water. He carried twin Colt Peacemakers with matched black gutta-percha grips. Every time the little fat man in the buckskin jacket threw a tin can high into the air from the bushel basket full of them he had on the platform, the man in black would draw one of the Colts, plug it five times while it was airborne, holster the Colt, pull its mate without missing a beat, and plug the can five times more where it landed, making it dance down the street, bang-clunk, bang-clunk, bang-clunk. Then he would reload both guns and go again. Always five cartridges, never six. Either he kept an empty under the hammer or he had something against an unloaded gun.

He was as fast as any man I'd ever seen.

"There you have it, friends and neighbors," announced the little fat man finally in a deep voice that carried over the echo of the last shot. "A demonstration in the fine art of pistoleering by its greatest living practitioner, Frank Willard, the Scourge of the Border, who single-handedly wiped out the infamous Turner gang at the Dodge station in eighteen and seventy-nine. Just one of the many stirring adventures that await your eyes and ears in Toby Shingle-decker's pasture this Sunday for the minuscule sum of fifty cents, children eight and under free. Shows at one, three, and five. See also Chief Knife-in-the-Belly of the murderous Blackfeet demonstrate the ages-old running of the buffalo and reenact the famous knife duel between Wild Bill Hickok and the Cheyenne Chief Black Kettle at Custer's battle of the Washita. Bring the entire family and treat them to a vanishing episode in American history."

Having unraveled all this in one breath, he filled his lungs again and started a pitch for something called Doctor Ernest's Nectar for the Treatment and Elimination of Ague, Catarrh, Toothaches, Bunions, la Grippe, Typhoid, and Halitosis. That same minuscule fifty cents, he promised, would secure a full pint of this miraculous elixir that would also restore old saddle leather to its original suppleness if you boiled the saddle in six parts water to one part Doctor Ernest's Nectar. We turned down a side street and could still hear the climb and drop of his voice when we reached the jail. The East had come to Helena, and it cost fifty cents a head.

THREE

Among the deputy marshals who rode for Judge Harlan A. Blackthorne there were three main evils, two of which had to do with the low pay and the standing order that deputies who brought their quarries in dead had to stand their burial. The third was the Judge's walk.

Four times daily, he strode the mile between his house outside town and the courthouse near the jail at a brisk pace that had been known to ruin some of the older deputies for the rest of the day after accompanying him. In the morning he made the journey to work, hands in his pockets and his large head sunk between his shoulders, nodding jerkily at citizens who greeted him, then reversed it at noon recess when he went home for lunch, made it again at the hour break, and walked home when the day's docket was empty, which most often was well after dark. Because all this walking carved considerable time out of his schedule, he conducted most of his business on the trot, with counsels and court employees wheezing to keep pace and hold up their end of the conference at the same time. Several lawyers and deputies had suggested he find a place closer to town—one at least had offered to build one—but the Judge always declined, maintaining that the walk was the only exercise he got. So far it had cost him three bailiffs, two to resignations and the other to a fatal heart attack.

The Judge was on the bench when I sent in a message informing him that I was back and that Sugar Jim Creel was locked up in Second Floor Felony. He sent a reply asking me to meet him in the courtroom at noon. Knowing what that meant, I made a quick trip to the room I kept over a harness shop across from the Belmont Saloon, took off my high-heeled riding boots, and tugged on a pair of farmer's brogans. I had taken my share of ragging from some of the other deputies when I'd ordered them from Montgomery Ward's catalogue, but that had stopped about the second time they came hobbling back from one of the Judge's walks.

I got to the side door of the courtroom just as it banged open and two deputies lurched out hanging on to a red-bearded, wild-eyed mountain man in a filthy bearskin and chains. He was struggling, growling in his throat like a cougar, and it was all they could do to keep a grip on his arms.

"How are things, Flynn?" I asked the older of the pair, a short, wide man with a band of black brow and handle-bars to match.

"About the same," he grunted. "You?"

"I found Sugar Jim."

"So I hear. They're whispering it in court already. Hear too you lost Dad and Rudabaugh."

I admitted I had.

"Reckon now we'll all pull a piece of their freight till the Judge finds two other dumb guys," he said. "Well, thank you all to hell, Murdock."

I got out of the way and the deputies scuffled down the varnished hallway toward the exit, their prisoner trying to crush them against first this wall, then that.

Cocker Flynn was the finest man who ever pinned on a star.

Judge Blackthorne emerged from the courtroom with a curt nod for me and continued across the hall to his chambers without breaking stride. The hem of his robes zinged against the floor. He was too short for them, though from a distance he didn't look it, he was that lean and wiry. There was still no gray in his goatee but there was getting to be plenty of it in his hair. Well, there was getting to be plenty of it in mine. At thirty-seven, when I had my hat off and the sun hit me right, I looked almost as gray as Dad. So I'd been told. Now that he was dead it was a toss-up between me and Cocker Flynn which one of us would inherit the old man's nickname.

I loitered in the Judge's doorway while he climbed out of his robes and into a black frock coat with beaver facing on the lapels. His clothes were his only extravagance. He ordered them from his tailor in Chicago and traveled there once every two years for a new fitting. All on his own money. He had no expense voucher and had refused Washington City's last two offers to raise his salary. It made Mrs. Blackthorne furious, but he had stopped listening to her years before I knew him.

He said nothing until we were outside, our heels knocking the boardwalk. He was wearing his black slouch hat and the porcelain teeth he put in only when he was working. They clanked on his *t*'s and *s*'s. "Let's have it."

I gave him it. The story didn't take as long to tell as I'd expected. He listened without interrupting, then:

"It could have been avoided."

"I'm sure it could have," I agreed. "Looking back on it, I can count three ways I should have gone. But I didn't have it to look back on at the time."

"You'll pay the court clerk two dollars for the man Melrose's burial. The government will eat the loss of Ruda-baugh and Miller. You were all taking the same chances."

"We buried Melrose out there. Besides, it was Ruda-baugh who killed him."

"But we can't fine Rudabaugh, can we?" He frowned a greeting at one of the town millionaires out strolling with a girl from Chicago Joe's. "The two dollars is punitive, as you well know. I have to make an example of you for the other deputies who otherwise will look at this and question why they're busting their rumps to bring in live prisoners when they can shoot them and be done with it."

"Sometimes it's worth the two dollars."

"To you, perhaps. Here it's four trips to Colonel Aaron Hookstratton's Frontier Extravaganza and Medicinal Demonstration."

"Who is he, anyway?"

"Ask him. He'll get around to introducing himself soon enough. Especially to you."

God knew what he meant by that. We had been together some time and I hadn't yet got the straight of him.

The town proper was behind us now. We were walking along the rutted road to the Judge's house with the broad brown soup of the Missouri on our left and beyond it the peaks of the Big Belt Mountains like dog's teeth gnawing a blue steel sky. White water threaded the middle of the river from the spring runoff. Some of the lower miners' settlements downstream would be flooding out about now, one of several reasons why I had never felt the urge to pan for gold.

The Judge had his hands in his pockets as always when he walked. Some thought he did this to avoid shaking hands with the people he met, but his marshal and deputies knew he carried a cocked .32 Remington in his right pocket. He'd been shot at once and scorned bodyguards. But he was a better jurist than a sharpshooter, and I always floated a step behind him when he was packing the little widow-maker.

"You've seen to the needs of those two deputies you recruited?" he asked.

"I put them up in the hotel. They're going back tomorrow. I told them you'll be sending them mileage and a courtesy fee in a week or so."

"They any good?"

"They're all right as guards," I said. "I wouldn't count on them for much else. The young one's living in a West that doesn't hold up outside New York and the old one's got a mean streak."

"You don't?"

"Mine's constructive. If we're talking about who I want with me when I go after the Indian and Harvey Byrd, I'll take Cocker Flynn and any other two federal men you can spare."

"You aren't going after the Indian. You're staying here to testify against Creel at his trial. I'm putting Flynn in charge of the manhunt."

I took some long breaths. This hike on top of so many days in the saddle was starting to make the tendons in my legs twitch like guitar strings. "You don't need me there. You've got half a dozen witnesses who saw him shoot the surveyor."

"I'm adding the murders of two deputy U.S. marshals to the original charge. You're the only witness to that act."

"I'll get a message to the kid at Painted Rock. He saw as much as I did. More."

"He'll be summoned. But your testimony as an expert will draw more water with the jury."

That was that. You argued with Blackthorne only so long and then you knew he had hunkered down like a buffalo in a blizzard and wasn't going to move. His house was in sight now, a two-story whitewashed affair with a colon-naded porch that was also a balcony. The grateful citizens of Helena had built it for the man who had come to a tent city with a copy of the United States Penal Code under one arm and a presidential appointment in his pocket before there was even a jail and set up business in a room behind one of the saloons where the prostitutes took their custom-ers at night. A hellhole when he found it, the city had been made the territory's third capital mainly through his taming influence and that of the men he had appointed to enforce the law. He hated the house, considered it pretentious, but his wife was comfortable there and though he wouldn't admit it he was flattered by the gift.

"I lost three more deputies to the silver strikes while you were gone," he told me. "That puts us at exactly half the strength we were this time last year. And Gordon's down with the gout again." Bill Gordon was the U.S. marshal assigned to Montana. "I wired the president to appoint a temporary replacement with power to deputize help. He's agreed."

"Who's he sending?"

"Jordan Mercy."

"Oh, that's just dandy," I said after a moment.

"He's a lawman. Gordon's a paper-shuffler."

"Mercy's a butcher, and a crook to boot. He'll deputize his brothers and cut himself in on all the gambling interests in town just like he did in Phoenix and Topeka. You'll do as well to spring Sugar Jim from jail and swear him in."

"I didn't swear in Mercy," he said. "The president did, or had it done for him months ago. In any case you'll do well to get along with him. Washington City wired him in Bannack and he'll be here day after tomorrow."

We paused in front of his porch steps. He never invited deputies or court employees inside, something to do with a promise he had made Mrs. Blackthorne early on about not conducting business in the house. I had started to turn away when I remembered the lynching. I turned back and told him about the two hanged men.

His brow grew dark. "Stranglers. They've been busy lately. Last month they strung up a sheriff up in the Bear's Paw, and two weeks before that a railroad detective outside Fort Benton. Likely there are more we haven't heard about yet."

"These two were John Does," I said. "You think it's the same bunch doing them all?"

"It had better be." He was using the bottom step to scrape dirt off the soles of his stout walking shoes. "Or we'll be dangling a lot more men from a proper gallows than we have in a spell. Don't forget to tell Mercy about this."

He mounted the porch and went inside. The Judge had a fiery temper, but he had learned to control it over the years. There were just two things left that could break it loose. One was any young lawyer from anywhere back East who thought he could slip a fancy courtroom tactic past the Judge's nose because they weren't supposed to know about such things beyond the Adirondacks. The other was lynching.

I made my way back to town on throbbing legs. It was starting to fill up with horses and wagons belonging to "morning miners," prospectors who picked and panned for three or four hours and knocked off at noon to drink and lie away the rest of the day in the saloons and hurdy-gurdy houses. The faces kept changing, because it was the ones who stayed out all day and never appeared in town except maybe once a week to empty a glass and pick up supplies who made money. The others tapped out early and went home saying that the only gold and silver in Montana was in the merchants' teeth. Piano music dribbled out of bat-wing doors and the balconies were blooming red and green satin and pink parasols. The faces under the parasols were getting younger and easier to look at, which meant the strikes were still good. It was when they got old and mannish that you knew things were sour. The young ones had the energy to go where the money was and the sixth sense that told them where it wasn't any more. They were always the first to know. The prospectors were always the last. But they kept walking around with their eyes on the ground when they should have been looking up at the balconies.

I spent an hour soaking off the dust in my favorite bath-house, a place ostensibly run by an apple-cheeked Irishman named Faolin who had left his foreman's job for the Great Northern Railroad when a sledgehammer crushed his foot, but that really belonged to an old mandarin who knew that not many white frontiersmen wanted to wash in water pro-vided by a Chinaman. I wasn't so particular. I got some of my best thinking done sitting in one of those scalding tubs with steam curling around my ears, shaving.

Contrary to what you may read, the time between inter-esting goings-on was generally a lot longer out there than it was in the East. Even when you were with the law you went a spell without getting shot at. I liked quiet, it was a thing I looked forward to coming back to when my lungs were full up with spent powder. But just now we had a boy killer in custody, a bloodthirsty Indian running wild, gold strikes east of town, silver strikes southwest of town, a four-bit Wild West show making things noisy in town, and stran-glers.

With all that, we hardly needed Jordan Mercy.

FOUR

Colonel Hookstratton's circus rig was still in the street when I came out in my city clothes, but there was no sign of its owner or his two companions. The mangy buffalo was still tied up at the hitching rail, its head drooping, too far gone to raise its tail and twitch off the flies buzzing around its shedding rump. It smelled like burning trash. A pair of morning miners in their twenties leaned on a porch post nearby looking at the beast. Red river clay clung to their boots and the knees of their overalls.

"Two of him wouldn't make a respectable cow," observed one, picking his teeth with a thumbnail. His partner snickered and spat into the street.

"Five years ago he'd have stomped your brains out through your ears if you tried to blindside him," I told the first.

He looked at me and said, "Yeah?" but he was just being polite to an old-timer of past thirty. The big shaggies were getting scarce even then. I went on to Chicago Joe's.

The place was half full of customers at the long back bar and at the tables opposite the varnished dance floor, their conversations brushing the rafters. The little stage where the three-piece band played was unoccupied, but their in-

struments were in place and there were two bartenders on
duty in white shirts and red sleeve garters behind a row of
brass beerpulls. A smoked mirror with a gilt frame and
some tasteful advertising signs depicting sparrow-waisted
young women in starched blouses and picture hats deco-
rated the wall behind the bartenders. The familiar, wiry figure of the Duke was visible to the left, immaculate as
always in white linen and black broadcloth, his gold watch
chain describing a glittering arc across his waistcoat. He
nodded when I caught his eye but otherwise showed no
expression behind the chin whiskers that hung to his cravat.
His polished British accent and dandified attire never in-
terfered with his handling of the staff and disorderly pa-
trons.

I bought a nickel glass of beer and took it to a table, and
two minutes later I had company. A twenty-year-old girl
with a pompadour of yellow hair and ruffled lace to her
neck looked down at me through a cloud of scent so thick
I could see it. "My name's Jackie. Would you like to
dance?"

I glanced at the deserted bandstand.

She said, "You could buy me a drink while we're waiting."

I asked where Joe was.

"She's in back. But she's old."

I said, "She's a year younger than I am. Anyway, it's
conversation I'm after. I'm just off two weeks in the company of men and you get tired of talking about guns and
horses."

"I can talk."

"You're too young. You'd dry up too quick."

She rustled away, ivory heels punching angry half-moons
in the floor's glossy surface. I sipped my beer. It tasted of
her scent.

Twice more I fended off female companionship. I really did want to talk to Joe. Right name Josephine Hensley, she had come out from Chicago in 1867 at the age of twenty-three with a string of girls and some notions of her own about how her type of establishment should be run. She had since moved from her original log building to larger quarters, taking her clientele with her, and when you wanted to know what was happening in town you bypassed the newspaper office and went straight to her. But today she was tied up with the books or something. I was about to drain my glass and leave when Hookstratton came in with black-clad Frank Willard in tow.

The Colonel spoke to one of the bartenders, who nodded in my direction. The pair looked over at me, Hookstratton curiously, his pet gunman narrow-eyed and dead of face. A look I knew too damn well. I made some arrangements with the Deane-Adams while they were on their way over.

"Page Murdock?" Hookstratton's baritone had the same mellow power at this reduced distance. The Mormon hat clung to the back of his head now and he had traded his gaudy jacket for a wrinkled black tailcoat and a swollen vest with cigar ash in the creases. Up close he had tiny, protuberant eyes, glass-blue, and a little triangular tuft of white in the hollow of his chin. A pattern of burst vessels made purple tributaries on his cheeks. He smelled of tobacco and whiskey and a good six weeks since his last bath.

I said, "Where's the chief?"

Confusion pouched his smooth fat face for an instant, then passed. "Oh, you mean Belly. He is outside. I fear he is not welcome where liquor is purchased and imbibed. I was not aware that we had made each other's acquaintance, sir."

"I caught a piece of your show outside."

"Just so. It is our humble lot to edify and to entertain."

"And to sell Doctor Ernest's Nectar for whatever's ailing you at the moment," I added.

He made a gesture of dismissal. "We have been carrying the same case of dusty bottles since last July. The public does not trust you unless you have something to sell. Forgive my Philistine manners. Page Murdock, Frank Willard."

I kept both hands under the table, not that the man in black had offered to shake either of them. His face was blade-thin under the Texas hat and badly pockmarked. He had a weak mouth and the intense, beady kind of stare you get from hours spent practicing in front of a mirror. For all that his eyes had a dull, empty look, and I realized that what passed for cool deliberation and lightning reflexes outside was just lightning reflexes with nothing behind them. My scalp moved.

"What can I do for you, Colonel?" I was watching Willard.

Hookstratton made a pleasant rippling noise in his throat. "Frank, another beer for the marshal, please, and the usual for me."

The young man in black measured me out some more of his dead glare, then removed himself, his shimmering boots making no noise at all on the floor. At the bar, yellow-haired Jackie saw something her age approaching and slunk forward to intercept him. He swept her hand off his shoulder with a vicious slash of his gun arm and kept walking.

"Your boy doesn't like women," I said.

With a grunt, Hookstratton planted his broad buttocks in the chair opposite mine, depositing a thick parcel swathed in ragged eastern newspapers atop the table. "He fears them. He is of the opinion they will drain him of vital energy."

"He's right. Where'd you find him?"

"Sweeping out the railroad station in Dodge for a dollar a week and found."

"That before or after he single-handedly wiped out the infamous Turner gang?"

His tiny eyes searched my face for a moment. Then he smiled, displaying a gold tooth behind his white handlebars. "One is allowed certain license in his quest for an audience. In point of fact, his only victims to date have been the occasional empty bottle and an incredible number of peach tins. So far as I am aware."

"Who taught him to shoot?"

"It is my understanding that he taught himself, employing an ancient Dragoon pistol whose cylinder he was forced to hold in place with his free hand in order that the hammer would strike the cap."

"A natural gunman," I reflected, watching Willard pay for the drinks. "I heard they existed. He's the first I've met."

"I observed him practicing behind the station, whereupon I took away his broom, gave him those Colts and that outfit, and began this tour. At the time I had but the wagon and the Indian and Caesar."

"Caesar?"

"The buffalo. God love you, lad."

Willard had returned with another glass of beer and a bottle of whiskey and a shot glass for the Colonel. He set them down on the table, spun a chair, and straddled it with his arms folded over the back, his blank eyes staring at nothing in particular.

Hookstratton filled his glass from the bottle, proposed a silent toast, and knocked down its contents. As the coppery flush came to his veined cheeks: "I'm told you brought in Sugar Jim Creel today."

"Me and some others," I acknowledged.

"Your modesty is misplaced. Your reputation has not eluded me in my frontier odyssey. You are often spoken of in the same breath with the late Mr. Hickok."

I sipped my beer and said nothing.

He topped off his glass again, drank off half of it, set it down, and undid the string on his parcel with a flourish. Parting the brittle newsprint, he thumbed something out of what looked like a stack of sawtooth paper inside and slid it across the table. It was a book with a brown paper cover, on which was drawn a crouched figure in black ink, a six shooter sneezing smoke and fire from his left hand. *Sugar Jim's Last Chance,* read the bold curlicued legend. *By Jack Rimfire.*

"Who's Jack Rimfire?"

He drew in his chin self-deprecatingly, sinking it in rings of suet cross-hatched with old dirt. "He is I. Or rather, I am he. The nom de plume has been made honorable by George Eliot."

I didn't know who he was either, but didn't ask. I flipped through the rough-cut pages idly. According to what was printed on them, Creel averaged fourteen shots to a revolver without reloading and could shoot with either hand and his teeth and pluck the eye out of an ant at forty paces.

"The style is a tad purple," Hookstratton apologized. "My readers expect it."

I slid the book back in his direction. "I'm glad I didn't read that going in. Appears I was lucky not to have to call in the army. How long have you known Sugar Jim?"

"We have not yet made each other's acquaintance. I was hoping to correct that situation on this visit. His arrest has greatly increased those hopes."

"See the Judge. Creel's his responsibility now."

"Just so. However, that is not what I am here to discuss." The musicians had returned to the bandstand and were tuning up their instruments. Hookstratton leaned forward, resting his fat forearms on the table and raising his voice above the plink-plunking of the piano and rusty squeals and squawks from the violin. "I do not intend to spend my declining years hawking medicine for the amusement of the soporific. I envision a grand prairie spectacle, re-creating under the broad blue skies the dash and grandeur of the frontier saga—mounted warriors in paint and feathers, charging ranks of cavalry, thundering herds of buffalo, the snap and rattle and bitter smoke of grim showdowns on hardpack streets between desperadoes and the guardians of law and civilization. I see souvenir hunters lining up forty deep at booths to buy signed photographs of the performers and literature telling of their real-life exploits. My vision includes performances in all the great cities of the globe, before all the leaders of the New and the Old World. A genuinely and uniquely American entertainment designed for international consumption."

"Sounds like a circus."

"Not the bogus vulgar inflation of the circus, but its exact and diametrical opposite: American history, retold as it happened, by the men who made it. Which brings me to you."

"I kind of figured it would."

"Mind you, this is not an overnight proposition. It requires patience and strict attention to detail. We will commence with a first-person account as told to Jack Rimfire of your capture of Sugar Jim Creel, a slim volume of, say, a hundred pages, but packed with action and the raw excitement of the hunt. More of your adventures will follow. Say, three months between them, to build reader suspense. Then when your name is sufficiently known we will stage a shooting contest between you and Frank in St. Louis or

Denver, publicize it heavily before the event, which of course will end in a draw. Then—"

"Save it for Toby Shingledecker's pasture," I said. "I'm not interested."

"Wait, you have not heard me out."

"I've heard my fill. Being a lawman makes me target enough. I have to walk on the shady side of the street now. If you make another Hickok of me I'll have to wait for sundown just to go out."

"The Colonel ain't finished."

I looked at Willard. He had a harsh whispery voice that cut through the music coming from the band. Joe's girls had latched on to some miners and were taking turns around the floor. They were admiring muscles and shambling footwork and didn't see the half-wit straddling the chair watching me with his hands curled at his ribs over the guns in his twin holsters. His eyes held that same burning look with only hollow skull behind it.

"Whistle him off," I told Hookstratton, without looking away from Willard.

The Colonel refilled his glass with a steady hand. "Frank is not offering an altogether unworkable compromise," he said. "Your demise would place the events of your life in public domain. I could then write the book and include an epilogue describing your unhappy fate. The Man Who Shot the Man Who Captured Sugar Jim is Byzantine billing, but acceptable."

"What about The Man Who Shot Frank Willard and Colonel Aaron Hookstratton?"

That took some time to seep in. The whiskey was dulling his brain even as it brightened his eyes. To help things along I cocked the Deane-Adams under the table. It made a noise like dried walnuts husks crackling underfoot.

"It's a five-shot revolver made in England," I explained.

"It's a forty-five-caliber double-action, which means that when the hammer's drawn back, like now, a kitten sneezing is all it takes to slap a hole through one or both of you wide enough to let through a buckboard and team. Whistle him off, Colonel."

He considered me over the glass in his pudgy hand. His chest, quilted with fat, lifted and fell. "All right, Frank."

Willard didn't move. Hookstratton said it again with a different inflection. The gunman lowered his hands to his thighs.

The band was playing "Clementine," the local favorite. I said, "You're breathing my air."

Hookstratton drained the glass and braced his hands on the sides of his chair. "Before we leave, I would admire to see this marvelous engine of British design."

I laid the slim gun still cocked atop the table carefully. Hookstratton nodded and pushed himself to his feet, a vein on his forehead swelling with the effort. Willard sprang up and slammed his chair back under the table.

"I would not have let this come to violence," the little fat man assured me. "I merely wished to observe your behavior under the circumstances. May I say that you behaved more than satisfactorily. Should you change your mind about my offer, we will be staying at the hotel through the end of the week. I would be honored if you would attend one of the Sunday performances as my guest."

"Thanks for the beer," I said.

He nodded again and turned toward the exit, swaying like a squat galleon in a high wind. Willard doglegged behind to keep an eye on me. The miners singing "Clementine" had finished with the standard verses and were getting bawdy. They'd missed the whole thing.

Helena didn't fit me right for a place to live anymore.

FIVE

"**W**atch your back, Flynn," I said.

I was sitting on one hip on the sill of my open
window, buttoning on my cuffs in the gray dawn chill and
watching Cocker Flynn leaning tight the pack straps on a
big army mule with a rippled white bullet scar along its
ribs. He had the two deputies from Great Falls with him
and a tall bony young deputy marshal we called the Swede
on account of his hacked-out features and pale hair and
eyebrows, but who was actually of English stock. They had
fresh horses built big to carry a lot of iron. At the sound
of my voice, Flynn spun sideways to offer a smaller target
and cocked a thumb back toward the scarred revolver butt
above his holster. Then he saw me and unwound.

"Watch your own," he replied.

That was the extent of our farewell. The Swede wound
the mule's halter around his saddle horn and the party
mounted and clanked away down the street, pushing mile-
long shadows ahead of them. Flynn and I had burned up
the first hour of the previous nightfall discussing the Indian's act of treachery and what he was likely to be doing
now and where he was likely to be doing it.

We both knew I was being punished for trusting too

much in Sugar Jim's drinking buddy. It was Blackthorne's policy to assign the deputy most recently familiar with the country to a manhunt there, and there was no other face you could put on my exclusion this time. Blackthorne tended to see things in dark and light. He wouldn't understand that you had to rely on the tools at hand in that place and in that time when men who knew the territory and who were willing to help out the law were so far apart you could kill a good horse riding from one to another. You took what you found and placed your faith in guns and God.

The Belmont started serving breakfast at first light for the miners on their way to their claims. I took bacon and eggs there and then checked the sorrel out of the livery stable and rode off the meal along the river. When I got back to my room I found a message from the Judge directing me to report to Bill Gordon's office.

Gordon was glad to see me. The marshal kept a neat little room lined with oak filing cabinets in the courthouse, and when I rapped on the open door he lowered a foot swathed in thick bandages from his rolltop desk to the floor and levered himself out of his chair with a stout cane. He was a middle-sized fifty with gray side-whiskers, gold-rimmed spectacles, and shoulders so stooped under the gray suits he wore he looked at first glance like a hunchback. His pockets were always full of papers and he never carried a gun and if you didn't see the plain star he had pinned to his vest you'd have taken him for a schoolteacher or a lawyer, which he was, both, long before someone in the White House thought he'd make a better lawman. He limped over to the door and snatched his derby off the peg.

"That it for today?" I asked.

"My foot says yes." The hat rested on his ears and on the tops of his spectacles. "I just came in to look at last night's mail and found him waiting for me to open up."

He gestured toward the bald man with a great noose of curly black beard covering his chest seated in the only other chair. "As if he didn't have an office of his own, and twice as big as this one."

"But only half as private. Hello, Murdock." The bald man unfolded his six feet four inches from the chair and reached an arm halfway across the room to take my hand in a firm grip.

"Mr. Springer." I found myself looking up at the carved-idol face with its great hooked nose and deep smoldering eyes, and as always when confronted with Judge Blackthorne's prosecutor I wondered if he bothered to wear a cravat behind that Homeric beard. As always I decided that he did.

"You hear who the Judge got to take my place?" Gordon demanded.

I said I had heard. He thumped the floor with his cane. "I reckon next he'll be deputizing Frank and Jesse."

"Don't blame the Judge," I said. "Blame President Hayes."

"I'll blame who I damn well want to. It'll take an act of Congress to fire me."

He stumped on out. Springer closed the door behind him, waved a hand toward the chair he had just vacated, claimed the marshal's swivel for himself, and spent some time arranging his legs as it was adjusted to Gordon's shorter ones. I took the other chair.

"The Judge has set Jim Creel's trial for next week," he announced. "I thought we'd go over your testimony."

"I've testified before. This is the first time you've called a rehearsal."

"Times are changing. Gold and silver has brought a lot of civilization to the territory over the past several months. The town is filling up with lawyers and every blessed one of them has been to the jail to see Creel. The lawyer who gets him out of this hole is on his way to a very lucrative practice.''

''Small chance of that.''

He smoothed his beard over his chest with both hands, a thing I'd seen him do in court when the opposition scored a point. ''You don't know these Eastern lawyers,'' he said. ''They'll tell you black's white and bring in precedent and a string of expert witnesses to prove it. I've seen slime swinging from gallows out here that would have walked away free as air back East. Men with even stronger cases against them than we have against Creel.''

''If that happens here, he'll be lynched sure.''

''Maybe not. His killing that government surveyor won him a lot of friends in the territory. Oh, and speaking of lynching.'' He drew a long fold of stiff paper from his inside breast pocket and handed it to me.

I unfolded it. It was a reader from Cheyenne directing all law enforcement agencies in Wyoming and Montana to watch for two Pinkerton agents reported missing during an investigation of the robbery of an Overland stage outside Rock Springs in December 1879. A detailed description of the missing detectives followed.

''That came in on top of a stack of bulletins with last night's stage,'' Springer said. ''The Judge wondered if those descriptions fit the men you found hanged.''

''They don't not fit them.'' I handed back the bulletin. ''Magpies and bloat don't help with identification.''

''If it was them and the incident is connected with various other lynchings around the territory, we're dealing with a group of vigilantes with a grudge against the law.''

''That narrows it down to three quarters of the population of Montana,'' I said.

He smoothed his beard. ''Well, that'll be Jordan Mercy's

first headache. What happened with the Indian?''

We talked until almost noon. He told me to speak clearly. He told me to sit up straight. He told me not to say anything derogatory about the court or my fellow deputies, as that might prejudice the jury in Sugar Jim's favor. I was to wear a clean shirt and a fresh cravat and watch my temper.

"I'm convicting a killer," I reminded him. "I'm not looking for a husband."

"Clamp a lid on your famous humor as well. Believe me, the jury won't appreciate it."

"Anything else?"

He peered at my face for a long time. Then he relaxed creaking in the chair with a long sigh. "Make an effort not to look so mean."

I got away from there feeling like a guitar string with too much turn to it and had lunch at the Belmont, washing down fried chicken and mashed potatoes with good wine. It didn't loosen my cramped muscles any. The saddle time and the tight airlessness in Bill Gordon's office were starting to tell. I walked around to loosen the joints and found myself standing in front of Chicago Joe's. I went inside.

Yellow-haired Jackie came over while I was drinking whiskey at the bar. Her blue satin dress hugged her trim hips and high bossed breasts so snugly that sitting down must have been a major operation. She had cut back on the scent today, and her natural coloring was as bright as the rouge on her cheeks. At least, that's how it seemed to me.

"I reckon you're wanting to see Joe and talk." There was a challenge behind her professional smile. Well, she'd been rejected twice the day before.

I said, "Nope," and ordered her a drink.

Later we had another.

When I hit the street after supper the saloons were going

flat-out, leaking yellow light and music and voices hoarse from calling for water in the sluices. Glass shattered somewhere, a silvery tinkle at this distance. Someone was enjoying himself this Saturday night. I felt no urge to join whoever it was. There was always a strained quality to the jubilance, a desperation to have a good time at the end of a full week of mule labor that would take on a nasty edge as the night wore down. I could see the city deputies being inconspicuous in the shadows under the porches. No matter how dark it got you could always catch light reflecting off their badges and the barrels of their sawed-offs.

Colonel Hookstratton's rig was nowhere in sight. He and his two-man, one-buffalo show would be squaring things away in Toby Shingledecker's pasture for the next day's performances. I wondered if I should accept the invitation to drop in. Frank Willard's six-gun witchcraft held a weird fascination for me. You couldn't do what I did and not feel the tug to watch someone else shoot. You never knew when he might be shooting at you.

"Marshal!"

At the whispered greeting I drew back instinctively into the shadows and looked around. There was no one on the street within whispering distance. When it was repeated I stepped out carefully and looked up. Jim Creel was at the window of his cell on the second floor of the jail across the street. A ghost of light from the passage behind him outlined his head clearly with his hands gripping the bars. He must have been standing on his cot, because the windows on that level were seven feet above the floor.

"Sugar Jim." My voice carried in the quiet of that narrow side street as if across water.

"Seen you coming out of Chicago Joe's before," he said. "Bet you was with Bertha."

"No, Bertha's too big for me."

"Jackie, then."

I said nothing.

"Sure, Jackie," he went on. "She's the first thing I look for when I'm in town. What you figure's the odds against a prisoner and the one who took him's being with the same girl?"

"Not so big. There's one woman to every hundred men out here."

"They's a damn sight less in here."

"Well, whose fault is it you're in there, Sugar Jim?"

"Oh, I ain't saying it's anyone's but my own." He paused. "This here's the first time I been inside, Marshal. Never thought it could be so hard looking at the sun shining and me not able to get out in it. Nor the moon neither."

"That's why it's called jail."

"Yeah. Well, I reckon I'll get out in the sun one of these mornings. Or are they doing that at night now?"

"No, they drop the trap at dawn usually."

"You'll not be sorry to see that, I bet. After what I done to your friends."

"They weren't my friends," I said. "You did what you thought it took to stay away from that morning drop. I don't know that I'd have done it another way in your boots. It's the Indian I want. He had a choice."

"He's a bad one, that Indian. He figured I paid better and quicker than the law, and I would of if everything had went the way it was supposed to. But I'd of got shed of him first chance. He's like a bee in a jar. You never know when you pull the cork who he's going to sting."

"Speaking of that," I said. "Why'd you kill the surveyor?"

"I got drunk."

"That won't sound so good in court."

"It's the truth."

I said, "No promises, but if you know where the Indian and Harvey Byrd are you might beat the rope. You're young enough to have plenty of suns and moons left after you put in your prison time. We're going to get them anyway."

Piano music clanked and clittered through the long silence. Then he moved his head from side to side slowly, and in the bad light I saw him grin. "No," he said, "I don't reckon I'll do that."

I resettled my hat. "I didn't think you would, Sugar Jim. I was just doing my job."

"What it takes," he agreed. "Going to see the show tomorrow?"

"I might."

"That fellow Willard is unchained hell with a Colt. I could of used him out there."

"You wouldn't have wanted him. He's as bad as the Indian, only in a different way."

"Being bad ain't fun. Don't know why so many folks figure it is."

"Being good's no walk in the flowers," I said.

The grin came back. "How the hell would you know?"

We said our good-nights. As I was walking away he started whistling that drover's ballad he'd made us crazy with most of the way back from where we'd captured him.

SIX

They rode sloppy, now abreast, now not, their saddle-bags flopping and slapping clouds of dust off their horses' ribs, but with a ragged discipline, as of the remains of a company of cavalry on their way back from a fierce battle. They were three big men in weathered black hats with the brims curled down in front and white linen dusters over their clothes, the tails split for riding and fanned out in back to cover their saddles. At first glance they looked alike, with their blue chins and thick black moustaches drooping over the corners of their mouths, but then you saw the lean muscles in the face of the man in the middle and the broad, double-chinned doughiness of his neighbor to the right and the pouty look of the rider on the other side with his lower lip outthrust. They all had the same straight nose and great brown eyes, the latter ringed dark.

Most of the faces that belonged to famous names out there were disappointing, no different from thousands of others in a place where severe weather and hard work and bouts with boredom shook out those men who didn't fit the type. The Mercys were something apart. Not outside the type, just more the type than the rest. Heads just naturally turned as they trotted down a boomtown street long accustomed to the tread of strange horses carrying nameless men. Their mounts were big roans, the man in the middle's a whiteface whose head looked like a naked skull until you looked again. All three were lathered and blowing.

I was watching the riders from the porch of the courthouse, where I'd just come off looking for a second morning's briefing with prosecutor Springer, only to find that he was in church. The sun was in front of them and their eyes were in shadow under their hat brims except when they raised their heads to scan the roofs and upper windows in that fashion peculiar to desperadoes on their way to tap a bank and lawmen on their way anywhere. Their plain stars showed flat and dull on their shirts where their dusters hung open in front. The curved butts of their Smith & Wessons were large and obvious with the dusters' tails pushed back behind them, and over their blanket rolls reared the oiled stocks of matching Winchesters. They looked like men going somewhere to do something, that was the difference. Though I'd never seen them before I knew them right off.

"Jordan! Jordan Mercy!" Colonel Hookstratton, coming out of the hotel next door picking his teeth with a sliver of gold, waved his hat. A perfectly round, pink bald spot the exact circumference of the crown glistened at the back of his head.

The rider in the middle, he of the lean muscles and skull-faced roan, turned in his saddle, fingers curling at his holster. His companions duplicated the maneuver an instant later like reflections in a slow mirror. When he saw Hookstratton, the first man crinkled his eyes and sidled over the boardwalk.

"Aaron, you old horse thief, have they not hung you yet?"

His voice was middle-register with a slight Kansas ricochet. His lips were drawn thin behind his moustache, and unless you were looking at his eyes you wouldn't have known he was joking.

"I had heard you were coming," Hookstratton announced. "These must be your notorious brothers."

The other two, still on horseback, had just joined them. Jordan indicated first the wide, doughy man, then the younger one with the little-boy pout. "Joshua and Jericho. Fellows, this is the Colonel Hookstratton I have been shouting about these past two years. The one who made me as famous as Sam Grant."

"An edifice is only as sound as its bricks." The Colonel expanded his great gut.

The others nodded but didn't offer their hands. That was another way you spotted them, by the way they kept at least one free all the time.

"You are still a drinking man?" asked Jordan.

"Who am I to deny a major industry its just profit?"

"I will take that as a yes answer." Jordan gathered his reins. "Let us attend to our mounts and then we will drink to old acquaintances."

"All the saloons are closed today," Hookstratton pointed out. "All those we should care to patronize, in any case."

"The bar will be open in Room Four at the hotel. Judge Blackthorne wired that he would hold it for me, and I never travel without proper supplies."

Jordan had turned back into the street and was slouching along toward the livery, his brothers falling into step behind. Hookstratton stood watching them for a moment, then wiped clean his gold toothpick with a white handkerchief and tucked the bright item into a vest pocket. He turned away.

"You know Mercy?" I asked him.

He started slightly and turned back. "Good morning. Yes, I met him in St. Louis in seventy-eight. My account of his adventures, *Mankiller of Topeka,* was published shortly thereafter and enjoyed a brisk sale from New York to Chicago. You might say with justification that I was the architect of his Eastern fame. I could do as much for you."

"I'll stand pat. Where's the Scourge of the Border?"

"Frank and Chief Knife-in-the-Belly are at the exhibition grounds rehearsing for the extravaganza this afternoon. Shall I look for you there?"

"I'm thinking about it."

"Give your name at the gate. My man there will be expecting you." He nodded thoughtfully, agreeing with himself, and walked away, his backside bulging under his tails.

I was still there a few minutes later when Springer came down the boardwalk, wearing a tight black Prince Albert and striped pants with a crease that would draw blood. His pearl-gray derby added unnecessary inches to his height. He asked me what I was doing there.

"You said yesterday we'd talk again tomorrow." I reminded him.

"I meant Monday, of course. I keep the Sabbath. Don't you?"

"I got out of the habit when I found out most of the people I was after didn't."

"It's your soul." He touched his hat and kept walking. He lived around the corner from the courthouse.

Sunday morning in Helena was a gray proposition. Chicago Joe's stayed closed by arrangement with the town council, the whiskey you bought in the only places that sold it that day was mostly Missouri River and chewing tobacco, and I had read everything in town except the Bible, and I knew how that came out. So I went to the livery for my horse and some exercise. The Mercys were coming out carrying their saddlebags as I was going in, their dusters

spreading behind them like capes, spurs going *ching-ching*.
They scarcely glanced at me as we passed.

"Mornin', Mr. Murdock," greeted the old Negro who
held down the stable, from the other side of Jordan's whiteface. "With you soon." He was rubbing down the horse
with a napless towel soaked in liniment. The air inside the
big dim building was sharp with the smell of it and of fresh
manure and rotting straw, like moldy newspapers bathed in
kerosene and blackstrap molasses. I told him not to hurry.

A spur tinkled behind me and I did a little side step,
trying not to look like a lawman getting his back out of the
line of fire. Now I was facing Jordan Mercy. His brothers
hung behind him, their broad shoulders carving big chunks
out of the square of sunlight framed by the wide doorway.

"I heard the black man call you Murdock," said Jordan
in his flat Midwestern twang. "Would that be Deputy
United States Marshal Page Murdock?"

I said it would.

His brown eyes scraped me up and down frankly. He
was about my age, with sun-cracks where his lids met and
windburned skin stretched taut and shiny over his high
cheekbones. His moustache was as dark as lampblack. He
said, "Your name follows me everywhere I go in the
Northwest. They say you are the man who put the snare on
Bear Anderson up in the Bitterroots. In Breen the talk is
you rode with Chris Shedwell just before he was killed,
and there is an army major in Dakota who is eager to talk
with you."

"I'll go back to Dakota when they move it to Colorado,"
I said.

"Mr. Murdock done brung in Sugar Jim hisself day before yesterday."

Jordan didn't look at the Negro. I could feel his brothers
watching me closely now. I said, "A kid I had along got

the better of him. All I did was sign him in at the jail."

"You will not get far talking yourself down that way. I am pleased to know you." The marshal started to introduce himself. I interrupted him.

"I know who you are. I heard you and Colonel Hookstratton talking before."

"Oh, you know the Colonel?"

"He's hard not to."

His eye crinkled. "Well, I *am* looking forward to working with you. What sort of boss is Judge Blackthorne?"

"He's a little like God. Only firmer."

Joshua, the heftiest of the three, chortled—a deep, phlegmy rattle. He was several years older than his more famous brother. "Sounds like you, Jord."

Jordan paid him no attention. "Are you going somewhere?" he asked me.

"Just unkinking my horse."

"Would you care to come to Room Four at the hotel afterwards? I have been rocking some fine whiskey since Bannack." He patted the saddlebag on his left shoulder.

"Afterwards I plan to watch Hookstratton's show."

"Yes, I should have guessed he would have one, this being Sunday. Maybe I will see you there, then."

"Maybe you will."

"Enjoy your ride."

He turned on his heel and went out. His brothers parted to let him through, then followed him.

The Negro finished with the whiteface and led it toward the stalls in back. "Nice gentleman."

"That's what everyone says the first time they meet him," I said.

SEVEN

Toby Shingledecker had fought the Sioux and northern Cheyenne to raise cattle on his fourteen hundred acres of grassland, then found that with wolves and sore winters and the high price of fodder he was better off running sheep. So he ran several thousand head of wool and just a hundred cattle, and called himself a cattleman who ran some sheep. A lot of men who had called him a sheepherder were walking around with busted faces. He was short, but his arms were long and he had no neck and his shoulders were as wide across as he was tall, and no matter how hard you hit him he didn't knock down.

Because he owned a manageable number of cattle, he was the only rancher around with a proper enclosed pasture of about six hundred acres strung round with barbed wire. That was where the Colonel and Frank Willard and the Indian called Knife-in-the-Belly and whatever other volunteer help they had been able to recruit had erected bleachers from a falling-down barn Toby had been meaning to clear away for years, suitable for seating two hundred spectators if no one got rowdy and brought down the works in a tangle of sharded wood and splintered bone. There was standing room for many more if they wanted to chance being charged by one of Toby's ornery bulls. The nearest of these was standing bowlegged several hundred yards off, grinding grass in its jaws and watching the activity with its horned head erect, when I got there and hitched the sorrel to the fence next to the other horses, wagons, and buggies. But the rancher had riders posted on the edge of the exhibition grounds ready to turn aside all bovine threats.

The bleachers were beginning to fill and there was a long line at a plank table laid across two barrels where Hookstratton himself was selling tickets. I recognized some merchants from town and a few miners and cattlemen in the line, but the rest were strangers, some with children still wearing their Sunday best. A lot of settlers had moved into the area since the last time I had been there long enough to take a hard look around. Chicago Joe was nearby, looking pretty in a solid, respectable way in dark green taffeta buttoned to her neck and a flowered hat among the more frivolous colors worn by her chattering girls under spinning pink and white parasols. She nodded to me with the tight-lipped smile she wore outside her place of business.

One of Toby's crew, a lean strip of hide in flannel shirt and jeans with flecks of gray in his moustache, was taking tickets at the gate to the pasture. Most of the workers on the ranch were past forty and getting old enough not to pick and choose between sheep and cattle work. He recognized me and let me through without asking for a ticket. Hookstratton had been true to his word. On my way past I nodded at the shotgun under the ranch hand's arm and asked him if he was expecting trouble.

"Colonel don't want nobody watching the show for free from the other side of the fence," he explained.

The circus wagon stood on the far side of the bleachers with its platform folded down and Frank Willard sitting on the edge, loading one of a row of six identical Colts lined up on the boards next to his hip. He had on the all-black outfit but not the Texas hat. The sun found blue streaks in his greased black hair. Caesar, the old buffalo, was tethered to the back of the wagon but the tether didn't look any more urgent here than in town. Files crawled in the bloody patches on its hump where the hair had fallen away in clumps. Its eyes were as dull and pulpy as skinned grapes.

Chief Knife-in-the Belly was doing deep knee bends this side of the wagon. Up close the Indian wasn't a Blackfoot at all, but a Ute, and dragging sixty behind him as fast as it dragged. His plaited hair was steel-colored and the skin on his face of knobby bone was as wrinkled as if a great fist had grasped it and squeezed. In a very few years his chin hooking one way and his nose hooking the other would meet. His breath came in short, heavy bursts through his nostrils, but his muscles responded smoothly and quickly as he squatted and rose, squatted and rose, again and again with his hands on his hips. I stopped counting at fifty and he was still going. He was naked to the waist, flesh sagging but strung with sinew like tough threads in a worn rug, and scarred like the buffalo was scarred, with thick ropes of white against his brown skin. He wore buffalo-hide moccasins and buckskin leggings, both darned many times, and a faded red breechclout that hung to the ground even when he stood. He was tall for one of his tribe, nearly as tall as Prosecutor Springer. His feathered bonnet was draped over the platform Willard was sitting on.

I spotted Judge Blackthorne's black slouch hat among a group of taller men in Stetsons and light topcoats under a cloud of cigar smoke, and since Mrs. Blackthorne—round and pink and stuffed into a russet-colored dress like a sausage in its casing—was chirping with a pair of women from town ten paces away, I joined her husband. Rumor had it that she didn't approve of me a lot more than she didn't

approve of any of the other deputy marshals who rode for
the court. When he saw me, the Judge abruptly turned his
back on the biggest mine owner in the territory, who was
in the middle of a joke involving a Chinaman and his Irish
mail-order bride, and smiled at me in that diabolic way he
had when he wasn't wearing his teeth. "Come for a
glimpse of the wild and woolly West, no doubt."

"I thought it might take my mind off my work," I replied. "I'm surprised you parted with the fifty cents."

"A dollar, counting Mrs. Blackthorne." His cigar had
gone out. He struck a match on his thumbnail and relit it
with none of the standard ritual, just stuck the end of the
cigar into the flame and let it catch fire as it would. Shaking
out the match: "Actually, we were invited by Colonel
Hookstratton free of charge. It was either this or suffer another visit from the Reverend Samuel Smithson and the
latest installment in the triumphs and travails of his brother
the archbishop. You've met the Colonel?"

"I met him."

"By your tone I take it we cannot expect to be reading
Page Murdock, Hell-Raiser of Helena this year."

"Nor any other, comes to that."

"I warned him he would find you a reluctant icon.
What's your reaction to this fellow Willard?"

"I wouldn't ask him to add one and one if I were in any
kind of hurry," I said. "On the other hand, I wouldn't step
on him when he was coiled either."

"So long as he confines his attention to tin cans and
bottles we'll not worry about how loud he rattles. How was
your session with Mr. Springer yesterday?"

"I passed fingernail inspection, but he's still concerned
about the backs of my ears."

"He learned his law in a rough school. I would listen to

him.'' He blew a perfect ring. ''I'm told Jordan Mercy and his brothers arrived this morning.''

''I talked to Jordan. I didn't get a chance to bring up that lynching,'' I added.

''No doubt you were too busy comparing me to God.''

I looked at him. He was watching Knife-in-the-Belly exercise. By now the Chief was well into the hundreds and was just breaking a sweat.

''You were unaware, apparently, of Mercy's penchant for gossip,'' said the Judge. ''You should know by this time that an animated tongue is the key to fame out here. Everything you said to him this morning is common knowledge.''

''I'll remember that.''

''Tomorrow morning, eight o'clock, my chambers. You, the Mercys, and I will discuss this strangling business.''

''Tomorrow morning I'm talking to Springer.''

It was his turn to look at me. I confirmed the appointment in his chambers. Nodding and smoking, he left me and took a seat in the front row of the bleachers, stopping along the way to pry his wife free of her companions.

''Seats, please, ladies and gentlemen!''

Colonel Hookstratton's powerful baritone rolled over the general babble. Conversations broke off and the knots of people on the grounds parted for the bleachers and places to stand on the edge of the arena, a two-acre section marked off by a ragged circle of Shingledecker men posted at its limits. There were four or five hundred spectators in the enclosed pasture. The man with the shotgun had turned away a hundred more at the gate.

I selected a likely fence post and leaned against it. The Colonel was alone on the grounds now, wearing his yellow buckskin jacket and the constant black hat. The Chief had finished his knee bends and was putting on the ornate warbonnet, tipping his head and the feathers forward, then back

like a turkey fanning its tail. The train swung around his
ankles. Frank Willard hopped off the wagon platform,
buckled on his gun belt, and twirled two of the six Colts
into the holsters.

Hookstratton began speaking. A gusting wind snatched
fragments of his introduction and shattered them against the
Big Belts to the east: "... exhibition of frontier speed and
marksmanship ... historic 'running of the buffalo,' sacred
to the Indians of mountain and plain, never before seen by
white eyes ... gladiatorial combat unparalleled since the
days of ancient Greece and Rome ... the winning and losing of the West in captivating microcosm ... American history, ladies and gentlemen, no mere shadow play or circus
trickery ..." His words growled like distant rifle shots in
the foothills.

It was a better show than I'd expected. Chief Knife-in-
the-Belly led off quietly with a demonstration of the
"Blackfoot," more likely Ute, death song, standing with
feet spread in the center of the arena, his guttural voice
rising and falling in that seemingly patternless cant that
never failed to lift the hairs on the nape of my neck, taunt-
ing the death-spirit to come for him, he was not afraid. He
was replaced at the end of his act by Willard, who galloped
across the grounds astride a white-stockinged black, a Colt
in each hand and the reins between his teeth, picking empty
brown Doctor Ernest's Nectar bottles off a row of fence
posts sixty paces away. The bottles burst with hollow plops
and left twinkling dust at the base of the fence. Caesar's
turn was next, and the old buffalo was the biggest surprise
of all. When the Chief first removed its tether the beast
didn't move and had to be shouldered this way and that by
the pinto Knife-in-the-Belly had between his legs until it
was in the center of the arena, where it stood hanging its
head, flies clouding its horns and rump.

"Ain't that there what's called a buffalo stand?" shouted a male voice. The crowd laughed and applauded.

The Chief was unmoved. Maneuvering his horse behind the buffalo, he brought up his six-foot lance and nudged the stone point into Caesar's flanks.

It might have been a bolt of lightning. The woolly beast threw up its head and let loose a bellow that shook the bleachers. Then the head went down and its back knifed up as if it had broken in the middle and both razor-sharp rear hoofs lashed straight back in a mule kick that would have crushed the pinto's chest had not horse and rider instinctively lunged aside right after the motion with the lance. As it was they had to keep moving frantically to clear the buffalo's circling charge as it swung around, horns down, hoofs pounding the earth and starting the low, rolling rumble once so much a part of everyday plains life. But the pinto was an experienced hunter and managed to dodge the swift, cutting passes and the treacherous looping sideways hook of the great horned head as the buffalo swept past, going "huh" through its nostrils with each heavy footfall. For those few minutes while the mounted Indian plunged and wheeled and threaded confusedly in and out of the bull's enraged maneuvers, Caesar was young and sleek and dark, a king in his world. Gradually, though, as its wind gave out, the buffalo allowed the enemy with the lance to nudge it by means of smart cracks on the right side of its hump and rump into a controlled loping circle with the Chief cantering alongside. It took the audience a moment to realize he was in charge. Then a pair of palms smacked together, followed by a crackle and then a roar of applause pierced by shrill whistles. The Chief steered Caesar out into the open pasture and rode with him until the buffalo's momentum flagged. After that the Chief used the lance to prod it back toward the wagon, where Frank Willard looped the tether over its drooping head. The flies returned to taste the blood on its tattered coat.

After the buffalo run, the advertised "duel to the death" between Willard in a hastily donned buckskin jacket as Wild Bill Hickok and Knife-in-the-Belly as Chief Black Kettle was almost an anticlimax, with the resultant "scalping" of the vanquished Indian as preordained as the whole sham battle was historically inaccurate. More than a few men among the hundreds watching tugged watches out of their Sunday vests during the five-minute pantomime.

Willard woke them up with another shooting exhibition, this time plucking coins out of the Chief's fingers from on foot at a hundred paces and snap-firing at peach tins hurled high into the air by the Colonel while the Chief kept him supplied with loaded revolvers from the arsenal on the wagon platform. The spectators hooted and cheered. Hookstratton waved for silence.

"Having billed Frank Willard as the fastest and finest marksman of our time," he announced, "I would be remiss not to offer the many other excellent pistoleers present today the opportunity to test their skills against his. I will pay five hundred dollars to the man who exceeds his score in competition here and now. Who will be the first to accept this challenge?"

The audience buzzed. Heads turned among the bleachers and in the gallery standing four deep along the edge of the arena. But no one came forward.

"Come, come, gentlemen. Surely there is one among you who upholds the higher virtues of shooting in this great young land of ours."

Still there were no takers. The Colonel strolled around the arena with his belly pushed out and his arms raised like a circuit preacher on the scout for secret sinners, wading through a pond of silence. He came to a stop facing me across a distance of less than thirty feet. "Perhaps," he bawled, "we can prevail upon that man of law and legend, Deputy United States Marshal Page Murdock, to lift the gauntlet I have flung down upon the fair earth of Helena."

There was a pause just long enough to measure my local popularity. Then the spectators fell to whistling and punishing their palms and stamping the bleachers, making them sway ominously.

"Go on, Marshal!"

"Show these boys how we do 'er in Helena!"

"Just pretend them tins is running away."

After that the language got mildly obscene for the Sabbath. I shook my head. The noise heightened. Hookstratton's low tones slid underneath.

"You complain about being a target," he said evenly. "If you turn me down you will give all your friends a reason to shoot."

"I don't have any friends here," I said.

"Does it hurt less to be shot by an enemy?"

Willard was standing at the wagon, reloading his guns with a flourish. He had gotten rid of the buckskin jacket after the Black Kettle act and was wearing the wide-brimmed hat, throwing his narrow face into shadow. The Chief, bareheaded now, squatted on his heels nearby with his wrists resting on his knees. Mainly, though, I was looking at Judge Blackthorne seated near my end of the bleachers. He was lighting a fresh cigar and not looking at me or paying attention to the commotion around him, which had started to take on a nasty edge.

It was the Judge who made up my mind. When you came to it, I did what he wanted me to when I was in his vicinity; it was a thing that went with reporting to his court clerk once a month to collect my pay. He set a lot of store by

his deputies' reputation in the community. Also he never
smoked two cigars in one day unless something was both-
ering him.

"Let's do it quick," I told the Colonel.

EIGHT

"The procedure is simple," Hookstratton explained.

We were standing in the middle of the exhibition grounds—Frank Willard, the Colonel, and I. The swell of cheers and applause that had washed over me when I stepped away from the fence had crested and broken and now the little fat man's astonishing voice rang out like a brass gong in the clear air.

"Chief Knife-in-the-Belly and I will, at our own pace, hurl one peach tin skyward at a time. The contestants will take turns firing, one shot to a turn, maintaining each tin in the air by the impact of their bullets until their cylinders are spent or the target is too low or out of range. Between volleys they will reload and holster their guns and draw them when the next target is launched. The contestant who misses, allowing the tin to strike the ground, has surrendered a point to his opponent. The first man with five points is the winner. As our guest, Deputy Marshal Murdock will fire first. Questions, gentlemen?"

Willard shook his head slowly, his sharp little eyes on me. He had heard the spiel before. I said, "It's clear enough."

"You have first choice among the weapons," the Colonel told me. "Every one of them is a triumph of precision engineering, manufactured expressly to my order by the Colt Patent Arms Company of Hartford, Connecticut. You may test them if you wish."

"I'll use this." I indicated the Deane-Adams in my holster.

"That is, I believe you said, a five-shot revolver. Frank is accustomed to firing five. You are welcome to load the chamber under the hammer if it is your custom to leave it empty."

"It isn't."

"Then let the contest begin. Chief?"

The Chief had just finished refilling the bushel basket with the plugged tins Shingledecker's men had retrieved from the arena. As Hookstratton joined him, he selected one and poised himself for a mighty underhand swing.

"Ready, gentlemen," said Hookstratton.

Willard and I put sunlight between us. I set my heels and dragged my palm up my leg and stood with it flat on my thigh. The first tin flew straight up and I waited until it reached the top of its trajectory and when it was hanging there, just before it started its plunge, I brought up my hand in a natural sliding scoop and the gun was in it and I thumbed back the hammer and pointed the barrel at the still-suspended target the way you would point a finger and pressed the trigger. The .45 barked harshly and there was an immediate audible clunk and the tin sped off at a sharp upward angle.

Someone in the bleachers started to yell, but the Colt in Willard's right hand spoke simultaneously and the can darted again in a flat spin. His draw had been a good fifth of a second faster than mine. I fired again, catching a piece of the tin and sending it out over the open pasture. That should have been the end of it, because it was almost out of range now and less than a handspan above the ground, but Willard aimed at hip level and shot and it jumped and it was my target again. I snapped off in a hurry. The can fell to earth without interruption. I had missed clean.

"Willard one, Murdock zero," announced the Colonel.

I thumbed out the spent cartridges and reloaded the empty chambers from the loops on my belt. Willard merely tossed his used six-shooter to the Chief for attention and transferred its mate from his left holster to his right. I made a mental note of the fact that although he seemed to shoot equally well with either hand, he preferred the right. You never knew when that kind of information might come useful.

When I had leathered the Deane-Adams, and while the Chief was reloading the fired Colt, Hookstratton removed a second tin from the basket and launched it without warning. But I was expecting something like that and plugged it ten feet out of his hand. Willard was then obliged to try and hit a target speeding away. He clipped it and that put it out of range. The one-nothing score stood. This time he replaced the spent cartridge with a fresh one, accepted the spare Colt from the Chief, and seated both in their holsters. His movements were casual, but he was breathing in short, shallow bursts. Well, so was I.

It went like that for a while, Hookstratton and Chief Knife-in-the-Belly taking turns throwing tins, now high, now low, sometimes barely letting us put away our guns before making us draw again. The cans Willard had plugged in his ear earlier demonstration were the most unpredictable, because they had been battered out of shape and had holes in them and some of them had spent bullets rattling around inside, making them wobble and dip unexpectedly. Also, the object quickly became not only to hit the targets, but to hit them in such a way that your oppo-

nent's next shot was close to impossible. It was like playing
billiards in the sky.

Willard missed twice, on our fifth and seventh rounds.
The first time he lost the tin in the sun. On the second my
bullet had ticked the edge of the peeled lid, spinning the
slightly flattened target so that his lead skinned past it without touching. That put me one ahead.

After that things got monotonous, with the pair of us
clunking the metal objects back and forth like shuttlecocks,
once keeping one suspended so long at an even level, hop-
ping in short arcs forty feet above the ground, that we both
ran out of ammunition and allowed it to plummet uninter-
rupted to earth. The audience applauded thunderously. I
was so busy congratulating myself I wasn't ready when the
next tin went up and hurried my shot and then we were
even again.

The intervals between targets stretched longer while the
bitter smoke cleared and our barrels cooled. My ears were
ringing. The spectators in the bleachers shifted their weight
on the hard boards. Some of the standees along the sidelines
sat down in their suits on grass still damp from last night.
Here and there jackets came off, the sun flaring off white
shirt sleeves. The first show was bleeding into the second.
The man at the gate had given up threatening crashers with
his shotgun and was letting them watch from outside the
fence.

The ninth tin left the Colonel's hand in a high, graceful
arc, flashing silver like a trout leaping in the sun. I led it
for fifty yards and started to squeeze off. A brittle hard
report shattered the air and the tin sped away.

I hadn't fired. Willard's Colts were still in his holsters.
We both looked to the right. Jordan Mercy was standing in
front of the bleachers with his feet spread and his Smith &
Wesson .44 smoking in his right hand. He was wearing his

black hat with the brim turned down in front and a black frock coat whose skirts flapped at midthigh. He had on a low-cut yellow silk vest with black fleur-de-lis and the ends of a string tie hung down evenly in front of a shirt so white it hurt to look at it.

While we were looking at him he fired again and then held the trigger down with his right forefinger while fanning the hammer with his left hand. They will tell you that you can't hit anything that way, but he buzzed off four rounds as fast as the cylinder would turn and the tin can danced in place and then hung there while his last shot echoed in the Big Belts. Then it fell.

Recovering himself with a twisted grin, Willard drew and punctured the tin square in the center at a height of fifteen feet. I was still holding the Deane-Adams. I hipshot, catching the target a few inches above the ground and sending it bounding across the pasture.

The mountains ground these last reports into a low hiss.

Colonel Hookstratton took advantage of the pause to waddle out into the arena and clap a soft pink palm on Mercy's shoulder. The marshal was busy shaking empty shells out of his revolver. "Ladies and gentlemen, it is my pride and pleasure to present Jordan Mercy, the Mankiller of Topeka."

There was another small silence while the audience absorbed this information, and then things got noisy again. The bleachers groaned beneath stamping feet.

"I think," continued the Colonel, when order returned, "that unless we are all prepared to remain here until dark forces us out, we may safely refer to this shooting match between Frank Willard and Deputy Marshal Murdock as a draw. The question at this point is whether one or both of our contestants will agree to a somewhat more demanding competition including Marshal Mercy. When in our lifetimes will these three gather again in one place?''

We looked at one another while the crowd shouted encouragement. Mercy's face was placid, Willard's tight and working, the deadly eyes aglitter, behind them hollow nothing. I don't know what my face was like. Whatever Judge Blackthorne wanted or didn't want was out of it now. It was a question of the newcomer's freshness against our battered eardrums and frayed nerves—assuming Willard had nerves—and which of us would back away first.

Surprisingly, it was Mercy. He had finished reloading and now socketed his big .44 in his high holster with nothing of Willard's flashy wrist action. "Another time, perhaps," he said. "Powder comes dear out here."

To say that Hookstratton was disappointed would be like saying Lincoln was dead. He attempted to change the marshal's mind by appealing to the audience, but it was already breaking up, half glad to be using muscles that had lain fallow too long. Mercy gave each of us a friendly nod and turned toward the gate, where his brothers were waiting for him. They had on suits like Jordan's, but only Jericho was wearing a yellow vest like his famous brother's. He was the youngest of the three and it was evident which of his elders he most wanted to be like. Their big roans were tethered on the other side of the fence with Jordan's whiteface in the middle.

Judge Blackthorne intercepted Jordan on his way to the gate. They spoke for a moment, shook hands briefly, and then the Judge returned to his wife, frowning a farewell in my direction before the shuffling crowd came between us. The Mercys went out to their horses.

Colonel Hookstratton sighed and made his way to the ticket table outside the pasture. Willard turned to face me.

"You and me again sometime, huh?" he said. "Without the tins next time."

Before I could respond he left me and reached into the wagon for a rag and a can of gun oil. The Chief was out helping Shingledecker's men scout up plugged tins.

I left behind the stragglers. Not a lot gained there that day, except the knowledge that Frank Willard was faster than I was but no better a shot, and that Jordan Mercy was faster and better than both of us.

NINE

Judge Harlan Amsdill Blackthorne had been born the first
son of an illiterate Missouri farmer, and so many of the
days of his life had started with the sun that his house was
always among the first around Helena to show a light.
When I appeared in his courthouse chambers a little before
eight the next morning he had already been there two hours
and cleared his desk of all paperwork his clerk had placed
there the previous night. Today he had on a deep burgundy
velour coat over a black vest with mother-of-pearl buttons
and a plain gold chain describing a blunted W across his
spare middle. Except when he was climbing into and out
of his robes I had never seen him in shirtsleeves. When I
entered he glanced up from the thick volume he had
propped against the edge of his desk and scowled at one
of the horsehair-stuffed chairs on my side. The wire-
rimmed glasses on his nose were a new development since
my last layover in town. I sat down and waited while he
read.

The room wasn't much larger than Marshal Gordon's
closet of an office, and smelled of mildewed paper and old
leather from the yellow-bound legal books wedged at various crazy angles into the tall cases against the north and

west walls. There was another much lower case under the south window that contained the works of Shakespeare and some newer titles, not so well thumbed. On the wall behind his desk hung a portrait of President Hayes and a bullet-chewed Mexican flag. The flag was a souvenir of the Montezuma campaign, but how among the thousands who fought in that war an eighteen-year-old volunteer had come to have it was something I had never been able to put together, and he never talked about that time except to complain that down there was where his teeth had started to go bad. He was fonder of reliving his one-man struggle against ignorance to pass the bar and his ramshackle early years as an itinerant legal counsel in claims disputes among the gold digs in California and the political battles he had waged on the floor of Congress that resulted in his assignment here. There was none shrewder on the subject of politics and none who had more contempt for it west of Chicago. He could paper his chambers with invitations to dine with the territorial governor that he had never bothered to answer. He had come here when the only law in Montana was measured in calibers, and with the gallows and a handful of hard men who had never before stood on the business side of a badge he had forced civilization down its throat. Whenever I got to thinking about what a bastard he could be I tried to remind myself of that, and of the battles he was still fighting with his enemies on both sides of the Mississippi.

I had been sitting there a full ten minutes by the grandfather's clock next to the door, listening to its click-clunking and the dry sibilance of turning pages, when the Judge closed the book with a noise like a pistol shot and boomed it down on top of his desk. "Have you heard anything of this?" he asked.

I craned my neck to make out the legend on the spine. *Ben-Hur,* I read. "No."

"You're fortunate. It's an advance copy from Lew Wallace's publisher. I knew the esteemed governor of New Mexico Territory down in Mexico and again in Washington when he was trying the Lincoln conspirators. As a lawyer he made a consummate soldier, but I never dreamed he couldn't write either." He peeled off his spectacles and looked at the clock. "He's five minutes late."

He meant Jordan Mercy, of course, not Lew Wallace. The Judge had a way of changing subjects so fast if you weren't listening closely you were caught short. But listening was part of what it took to stay alive in my work, and I said, "Maybe he was up late counting his take from the Belmont."

"He'll not try extortion here. This isn't the kind of canvas cow town he's used to."

"That's what they said in Phoenix. Inside of a week he had a piece of everything in town."

"I'd be interested in knowing how."

I almost asked him if he had plans of his own along those lines, but you never knew how healthy the Judge's sense of humor was on any given day. "It's legal, up to a point," I said. "Every town has its ordinances, and you can expect just about every business that's worth looking at is violating one or two of them. I've never seen Mercy at work, but if he does it like some I've seen, he threatens to close those places down on those grounds unless they kick in to him."

"Which is when it stops being legal."

I said, "Say you own one of those businesses. Where do you go to complain? Mercy's the law. Refuse to go along and he and his brothers come in with their guns and maybe an axe and close you down for good."

"He's not the law here. I am."

"You and that thirty-two pistol in your pocket. His is a forty-four and you saw yesterday what he can make it do."

"He'll not try it here," he repeated. "Even in our present deplorable state of manpower it would be like robbing the Denver mint. If, however, he should be foolish enough to make a liar of me and stand the attempt—"

I assured him I'd use discretion.

He said, "Discretion, hell! Arrest the son of a bitch."

Someone rapped on the door. The Judge barked an invitation and Jordan Mercy entered. He was wearing the same suit and fancy vest he had worn to Shingledecker's pasture.

"What son of a bitch is that, sir?" he asked, when greetings had been exchanged.

"Someone involved in a case that has nothing to do with this meeting," snapped the Judge. "You're late. Where are your brothers?"

"I thought it wise not to have us all in the same room at the same time. Shortly before I arrived in Topeka, a powder charge thrown through a saloon window killed the town marshal and two of his deputies. When I got there I had to wire for Joshua and Jericho to come help. I had nothing to work with."

"Before we go any further, let's get square on who makes those decisions in Helena." Blackthorne was sitting straight as a schoolmaster with his blunt-nailed fingers on the near edge of the desk. "Listen. Can you hear the voice of democracy in this room? If you say you can you're a liar, because you can't hear it this far from Washington. When I make a direct request of an employee of this court, it is not open to interpretation. Flout it for whatever reason and, believe me, you'll think that powder charge in Topeka was someone belching. Would you have that clearer?"

You had to admire the Judge's control. The town still

talked about the time in court he grabbed a young Virginia
attorney by his cravat, no one remembered for what infrac-
tion, and pistoned his fist into the captive's face three
times before letting go and allowing him to dribble down
the bench into an unconscious puddle on the floor. But that
had been early in the Judge's tenure, before he had learned
to harness his rage, and now there was just the thrum of
iron in his tone.

He and Mercy watched each other, the latter motionless
except for the play of muscles beneath the skin of his face.
It had been a while since anyone had spoken hard to him;
that much lay right on top where you could look at it. The
last time would have ended noisy. But in that close book-
lined room with the torn flag on the wall and the little chin-
whiskered man behind the desk there was something like
the unseen thing that forbids laughing in church. Finally
the brim of Mercy's hat moved down and up slowly. "It's
clear."

They were almost the same words I'd used when Colonel
Hookstratton had explained the rules of Sunday's shooting
contest. Something left then, and Blackthorne sat back.
"We'll not waste time fetching your brothers in here. I'm
in court in forty-five minutes. You'll have to fill them in
later."

He indicated the chair next to mine. The marshal hesitated, then removed his hat and sat down, hanging the hat
on his crossed knee. His hair was the same even black all
over, though not glossy like Frank Willard's, and receding
along both sides of a sharp widow's peak. There was a band
of fair flesh across his forehead where his tan quit.

The Judge offered him a cigar from the humidor on his
desk. Mercy accepted it and bit off the end and took it out
of his mouth and found the wastebasket and got rid of the
end. He let the Judge light the cigar, turning it in the flame

of the match, then settled back and shot smoke at the ceiling. I took advantage of the pause to get up and crack the window. It was a small room like I said, and I don't smoke. I sat back down.

After a curt preamble from Blackthorne I told Mercy about the two men found decorating a tree during the Creel chase. The marshal listened with what looked like interest.

"We think they might have been a pair of Pinkertons that came up missing while tracking a gang of stage robbers from Wyoming," added the Judge. "There's a chance this lynching is connected with two other lawmen hanged in that same general area last month."

"Vigilantes?" suggested Mercy.

"Or just a gang of hotheads," I put in. "They don't hold us in high regard in that country."

"They get impatient waiting for justice up around there, I guess."

"They'll know justice on my gallows," Blackthorne growled. "I want you and your brothers to ride up there and ask some questions."

Mercy drew in a lungful of smoke, held it, and let it curl out under his moustache. "We will not get answers out of their like."

"Perhaps not. But it's important the questions be asked. Lynch law passed out of fashion in Montana when I accepted this appointment. I want them to know that up there, and also to know I mark the sparrow's fall in my jurisdiction."

"I was told you have men up there now."

"They're on a different manhunt. It would slow them down."

"Is that why you called us all this way? Why can't you send Murdock?" He spoke bitterly around the cigar clamped in his teeth.

"Deputy Murdock is testifying in court Wednesday."

"I didn't pin on this star to run errands."

"You pinned it on for forty a month and six cents per mile." The iron was back. "If you counted on more I'll trouble you for it."

Mercy rose, killing the cigar in the heavy brass ashtray on the desk. "When do we leave?"

"Whenever you can," said the Judge, expansively. "You'll want a packhorse and supplies, as this may take a while. See my clerk for expense chits."

"Tomorrow, then. First light."

"First light tomorrow will be fine."

"That it?"

"Unless you have something else to discuss."

"No," said Mercy, glancing from the Judge to me. "No." He left us.

"That's an unhappy man," I said.

"Indeed." Blackthorne pushed out his cheeks in a burst of air. "Did you notice toward the end how he stopped talking like a character in a novel?"

"He had plans that didn't include leaving Helena for a while."

He studied my face. "Maybe. And maybe he's just been giving orders so long that taking them doesn't fit any more." He glanced at the clock. "Mr. Springer's waiting for you in Marshal Gordon's office."

I got away from the prosecutor a little before eleven. He was due to relieve his assistant in court at the end of the noon recess and he wanted to have lunch and then confer with the Judge during the latter's walk home. While I was walking along the boardwalk breathing the sweet outdoor air, three pairs of spurs came up behind me with a noise

like coins banging around inside a jar. At the end I turned
sideways and nodded at the three Mercys.

"You have eaten?" Jordan inquired.

I said I hadn't. He said the Belmont served a fine free
lunch and I said I knew that and he said he would like to
buy me a beer and I said that sounded pretty good and the
group headed that way.

The saloon was almost deserted at that time of day. We
ordered four beers and four roast beef plates and retired to
the curtained alcove where poker was played evenings.
Joshua, true to his girth, was the most serious eater of the
family. He hung his frock coat on the back of his chair,
removed his cuffs, and tucked his blue-and-white-checked
napkin inside his collar before digging in with his knife and
fork. Young Jericho poked at his potatoes as if he expected
blood to come out. He looked disappointed when it didn't.
I was starting to feel about this quietest of the brothers the
way I felt about Frank Willard. His face had a girlish look,
his complexion like roses and milk under the superficial
tan. He had very long lashes and his thick, sullen lower lip
was as red as rouge. The fine black moustache looked
pasted on. I didn't have a handle on him and wanted one.

Jordan sawed off a piece of beef, chewed it throroughly,
and swallowed before speaking. "I see what you meant
before about the Judge."

"He does his job his way." The meat tasted salty. I
washed it down with beer.

"I fail to see how you put up with him," he said.

"Most of the time I don't have to."

"Yes, I thought your skin was too burned for town life.
You know your way around a gun."

He waited, expecting me to return the compliment. Instead I said, "Did that surprise you?"

"Not really. You have the look. But there are a considerable number of men walking around with guns in this country who can barely remember which end the bullets come out. Josh thought you were just another dandy."

I glanced down at my town clothes. My collar was growing hair and one of my shirt buttons didn't match the rest. With his mouth full Joshua said, "I meant that iron of yours. It looks like a walking-around piece, not something you shoot." He drained off half his beer and licked foam off his walrus moustache. Grease plastered down the hairs.

"It's the second one of these I've had," I said. "I lost the first in Dakota. The cowman who brought me up willed it to me when he was dying with a Cheyenne arrowhead in his liver."

"Not much to leave a person," Jordan commented.

"He didn't have much to leave. We seem to be using up a lot of time talking about one gun."

"I guess when schoolteachers get together they talk about books just as much." Jordan touched his lips with his napkin and pushed his plate away. "We could use a man like you."

"I thought we had a man like me already."

"I mean Josh and Jer and me. While you and I were with the Judge I had them scout out the town. Helena is a rich place. You don't often see this many brick buildings where wood is so plentiful and cheap. Enough gold and silver comes through the assay office each week to fill a train you will not want to wait for at a crossing. Most places, you look at a man's clothes to learn how well he is off; here you look at his pockets. Every other miner has his overalls stuffed full of ore samples. Chicago Joe must clear a thousand a month just from the gold dust spilled in the cracks of her floor and answers to no one for it. There is so much money here they play with it the way an Indian strings double eagles around his neck because they look pretty.''

"This m-morning I seen two guys b-bet f-f-five hundred b-bucks on whether a b-bird sitting on a telegraph wire would f-f-fly west or east when it lit out,'' volunteered Jericho.

He stared down at his plate as he spoke. I knew then why he kept silent most of the time. I said, "Which way did it fly?''

The youngest Mercy glanced at me swiftly, and something like a grin briefly turned up the corners of his moustache. "S-south.''

"The point being,'' Jordan cut in, "that it is high time someone showed these people the value of their money.''

"By taking some of it away from them,'' I finished.

"It is not as if we were offering them nothing in return. Security has its price.''

"They pay it through licensing fees now.''

"It is a poor figure for the risks we are taking. A town with this many growing concerns should not have to yield more than twenty dollars per merchant each month. It would mean a substantial income for each of us on a regular basis.''

"Thanks, but I don't spend what I'm getting now.''

"Then save it. When statehood comes you will have enough to buy into the governorship.''

"That sounds like your dream, Mercy. It sure isn't mine.''

He ran a polished nail around the thick lip of his glass, making it ring dully. "The frontier cannot last,'' he said. "The time is coming when men like us will no longer be needed or wanted. Where will we end up? Swinging a stick on a street corner in St. Louis or plugging peach tins in a show like Colonel Hookstratton's. Now is the time to feather our nests, while we still have strength to lift the feathers.''

"Talk to Frank Willard.''

"He is all hand and no head. Any fool who practices can draw a gun fast and hit what he aims at. Shooting at targets that may shoot back requires something more. You have to make your mind up before you leave the house that you are going to kill someone today, and you have to do that every day because you never know which day you will be called upon to keep that promise. It requires a man with his senses about him. I am telling you nothing new.''

I slid my knife and fork onto my plate and emptied my glass. "I'm not sure I could get used to collecting taxes at gunpoint. I appreciate the beer. I haven't had to buy one since I got back to town. Everyone keeps making me offers." I rose.

Jordan leaned forward and caught my wrist. "If you will not stand with us, I hope you will not stand in front of us.''

He was looking up at me with nothing but sincerity in his doe eyes. The others had stopped eating and drinking. Their hands were out of sight under the table. I removed Jordan's hand gently, nodded to his brothers, and went out through the curtains.

"I told you, I got business with Mr. Murdock.''

The voice in the main room came from the batwing doors, where the bartender, a former prizefighter from Denver, blocked the way with a short solid length of pool cue in his broken-knuckled hands. "I don't care if it's with Paddy bloody Ryan. No niggers in the front door.''

The old Negro who ran the livery stable caught sight of me over the bartender's side-of-beef of a shoulder. "Mr. Murdock! They said you was in here.''

Call it reaction to the scene with the Mercys or plain

lawman's instinct, cold iron stroked my spine to the base of my neck. I asked him what he wanted.

"I done tried to talk to the Judge, but he's in court. Cocker Flynn's horse, he done come back to the livery just now. Without Mr. Flynn. Saddle's got blood on it."

I shoved the bartender aside the way twenty-three fighters in their prime had failed to do, and outran the Negro to the stable.

TEN

I found him three miles outside town, lying alongside the same road he and the Swede and the two sheriff's deputies from Great Falls had taken two and a half days earlier on their way to find Harvey Byrd and the Indian.

At first I missed him. There was the unusual amount of tree fall cluttering the landscape after a hard winter, and in the dull browns and grays that Flynn wore on manhunt he looked like just another toppled-over stump in the tall tan grass. I passed by him with hardly a glance, but then the iron touched my back again and I turned the sorrel and there was Flynn's dented Stetson resting crown-down on top of a fresh gopher mound as if he had laid it there while he took a nap. I stepped down and knelt and placed my hand on the back of the short wide man stretched out on his stomach with crickets crawling over him. I could feel the pumping of his strong heart through his shoulder blade, straining more than ever now that there wasn't as much left to pump. I slid the hand under him to turn him over gently and felt the thick warm stickiness matting his coat and shirt to his side and bile climbed my throat, bitter as decayed lemons, but I swallowed it and got him on his back, and against the pallor of his features the startling black of his hair and eyebrows and handlebar moustache, blacker than either Willard's or Jordan Mercy's, looked like what undertakers do to corpses to make them look less dead. It never worked with them and it didn't work with Flynn. But he was breathing. You could hear it across the road if you were listening for it.

The Negro arrived with a wagon from the livery while I was stuffing a wad of grass into the hole in Flynn's side. He grunted from the pain of it, but for the most part he was somewhere I couldn't reach him. "Where's Doc Chrichton?" I asked the Negro when he joined me.

"Splinting a busted leg out at the Dumphrys'. Young Jake fell off'n his horse again. Mrs. Chrichton, she said he likely be back by the time we get to his office."

We got the wounded man into the back of the wagon and I covered him with a blanket the Negro had brought and I mounted up and the Negro climbed into the driver's seat and we made our way back to town at a painful pace, the Negro trying to find a road among the ruts without pitching his passenger out of the bed.

Doc Chrichton was younger than you usually found them out there where most patients paid in chickens or worthless mining stock when they paid at all. He had a lantern jaw and blue eyes and very light brown hair hanging in wings on both sides of his forehead from a natural break in the center. His wife, a tall woman four years his senior, dark-haired and hard-faced, was a nurse. They met us in front of their house just inside the city limits and the doctor helped us carry Flynn inside while his wife held open doors. We passed through a sparsely furnished but neat parlor that doubled as a waiting room and then through an office smelling of iodine and alcohol into another room containing a cot at the back of the house. When Flynn was on the cot, Mrs. Chrichton started rolling off his clothes while her husband removed his own cuffs and washed in a basin full of steaming water. I asked him what he wanted us to do.

He wiped his hands off on a clean towel. "Close the door. From the other side. If we need you we'll call you."

A glass-fronted bookcase stood in the parlor, its shelves crowded with matched sets bound in brown leather and lined up like logs in a stockade. Medical books, an encyclopedia, the usual Shakespeare, Boswell's *Life of Johnson.* "That there's a fine book," said the Negro while I was studying the last.

I looked at him. The skin of his face was the same shade as the leather bindings and drawn into sharp straight creases like old cloth folded away in a trunk. His short coiled hair was the color of granite and his shirt and jeans were just things to cover his thick hard body, faded and glazed with sweat and dirt to an even gray. I said, "You can read?"

He unwrapped a shy grin with six teeth in it. "A man that owned me had a sick son. He teached me to read so's I could read to the boy when he wasn't home. I read him Boswell and most of Shakespeare and some of *The Decline and Fall of the Roman Empire,* and then he up and died and I got sold. I never did get to find out how that fellow Attila made out."

There was a history of Rome on the bottom shelf. I tossed it to him and took Boswell for myself and we made ourselves comfortable in a pair of worn leather chairs with hollows in the seats.

I was up to Dr. Johnson's correspondence with Edward Cave when the door to the office opened and Doc Chrichton came out fastening his cuffs. He had been with the patient almost two hours.

"The bullet transfixed his left side and came out the back," he explained. "It cracked a rib on its way through, but that's minor. I flushed the wound and patched him up front and back. Which one of you plugged the entry hole with grass?''

I told him I did.

He nodded. ''You greatly increased the risk of infection. But you did slow down the bleeding. Otherwise you probably wouldn't have gotten him here alive.''

''Will he make it?''

''He's lost a lot of blood. He shouldn't have made it as far as he did. But he has the strongest heart of anyone of his age I've seen. Barring infection, his chances are fair to good.'' He paused. ''He wants to see you. I said no, but he threatened to rip out my dressing. Make it fast.''

On my way through the office I stepped aside for the doctor's wife coming in from the back room with a tray full of bloody instruments. She said, ''Isn't there enough sickness around without you men slinging lead at one another?''

''I didn't shoot him,'' I said.

''You've shot others and made more work for other doctors and not a few undertakers. I saw you out there yesterday playing with guns. What's there to be proud of in being able to kill faster and better than anyone else? I hate guns.''

''They're just pieces of steel. You can't hate them or love them. Hate the people that make us use them.''

''I hate all of you,'' she said. ''That way I don't have to waste time sorting you out.''

I let her world turn her way and went into the back. Cocker Flynn was lying under a thick quilt and alcohol fumes heavy enough to cut a slice out of, with his hair plastered to his forehead and his eyes closed. At first I thought he was asleep, but when I was standing over him they opened.

''What you looking like that for?'' he demanded in a

voice I could barely hear. "I'm the one got shot."

"Who shot you?"

"It was dark as hell. I didn't see them."

"How many were there?"

"Well, if it was too dark to see who it was, don't you think it was too dark to count them?"

"Calm down and tell me about it."

It took a while. I had to hunker down and place my ear almost to his lips to make out most of it, even then I lost some of the details when his voice receded entirely before swelling back up, like an argument in a house across the street. The way I pieced it together, Flynn and the Swede and the two deputies from Great Falls were setting up camp in the Smith River country just past dark their first night out when a large band of mounted men came up on three sides of them with rifles glimmering in the starlight and told them to throw down their weapons. Someone—Flynn thought it was one of the men from Great Falls—made a move and the mounted men opened fire. Flynn hooked out his Colt and rattled off three shots at high shadows, but by then bullets were singing all around him and he dived under the pack mule, nearly getting stamped to death when lead struck one of the packs and the animal brayed and started bucking. It wasn't until he was on the ground and feeling for more ammunition on his belt that he felt the wetness on the side of his shirt and realized he'd been shot clean through. He was sorry he'd found out because right after that he started to hurt and get weak.

The shooting was still going on. It seemed like a long time, but when he thought back on it afterward and counted the seconds, the total kept coming up less than a minute. Someone flopped down at full length right in front of him with a grunt. He thought it was the Swede. The gunfire stopped then, and the next few moments were filled with

boots crunching on the frosted grass and indecipherable
mutterings. By this time Flynn was floating on the edge of
unconsciousness, so he couldn't be sure if he heard what
he thought he heard next or dreamed it, but someone—it
sounded like the younger man from Great Falls—called
someone else a son of a bitch, and right after that there was
a loud crack as of an open hand slapping someone's face
hard. He didn't hear the voice again.

A male voice he didn't recognize called for a light. A
horse whickered and leather squeaked and metal rattled,
followed by a creak as of a lantern glass lifting, and then
a match popped and flared and greasy light slid across the
ground in front of Flynn. A pair of boots wearing cruel
Mexican spurs jingled forward and stopped next to the
fallen Swede. Just then the Swede's gun came up, but one
of the boots kicked it flying and the broad muzzle of a rifle
struck bone with a thump. The Swede grunted and lay still.

"This one's breathing," the man with the spurs announced. "Think I busted his skull, though."

"What about the other?" asked the man who had ordered the light.

The spurs came Flynn's way. He shut his eyes and held
his breath. Clothing rustled and something touched earth
close by and he felt the heat of the lantern on his face. He
was lying with his head turned sideways. A hand smelling
of tobacco and spent powder touched his face and he rolled
his eyes as far back as they would go just before a thumb
pried open his right eyelid.

"This one's dead." Spurs let the lid drop.

"One less rope, then," said the first man.

"Bury him?" This was a new voice.

"We bury any of the others?"

There was no reply. The first man said, "Get his gun
and let's go."

Flynn's Colt was slid from under his hand. Surrounded by men with guns, he made no attempt to hold on to it. Spurs rose. The lantern went up with him and the deputy started breathing again, trying not to gasp.

"What about the one with the busted head?" Spurs wanted to know. "He's got a bullet in him too."

"That don't mean he won't swing just as good," said the first man.

Two of them bent to drag the unconscious Swede to his feet. Flynn blacked out then. When he came to, the sky was going pale and something cold and moist was rubbing the back of his neck. After a moment he realized it was his horse. It must have run off during the shooting and wandered back after the others had gone. His memory wasn't reliable on the rest of it, but somehow he had managed to pull himself into the saddle and make his way back to Helena and help, depending as much on the horse's homing instinct as on his own eroded abilities through that day and most of the next night, until weakness and gravity got the better of him and he tumbled out of the saddle and hadn't the strength to climb back up. The horse had waited around for a while, trying to rouse him by rooting its muzzle under his arm, then had given up and trotted riderless the rest of the way home.

I was trying to get some more details about Flynn's attackers out of him when the doctor came in. "That's enough," he snapped. "If it's killing him you want, you'll not do it here."

I told Flynn I'd be back to visit him and went out. The Negro was reading about Attila in the parlor. He closed the book and stood.

"The bastard was born to die of old age," I told him. He flashed his gap-toothed grin.

I had twenty dollars in paper money in my poke. I held

it out to him. "It's not near enough," I said. "You bought him a lot of years today."

"It's too much, Mr. Murdock. You better keep it."

"I'm not trying to buy you."

"I know. I pull out paper like that anywhere in town, folks just figure I stole it."

I hadn't thought of that. I put the money away, then thought of something and fingered the dented star out of my shirt pocket and held that out.

He grinned again. "A black marshal?"

"If you ever need me and can't get to me, send that. I'll come as far as I have to."

Still he hesitated. "Don't you need it?"

"I haven't so far."

He accepted it then, polishing it on his sleeve before buttoning it away in one of the flap pockets on his breast. On our way out of the house I asked him his name.

"Duncan," he said.

"First or last?"

"Both. First man that owned me gave me his last name as a kindness, but I never taken to it."

He held the door for me and we stepped out into the sunshine. "How'd Attila come out, by the way?"

"He done lost." He shrugged a corded shoulder. "They always do."

"Only in books," I said. We parted.

ELEVEN

It was warm in the courthouse. The side door leading into court was propped open to create a cross draft through the main entrance, with the Judge's bailiff, a tight old former deputy with a horseshoe of white hair around his naked scalp and a forked beard, sweating in the slow current of air from the hall. Behind him a clerkly man in a black suit sat in the witness chair explaining to the jury in conversational tones how he had come to split open his wife's face with a horse collar.

"Judge can't be disturbed while court's in session," the bailiff told me. The plain butt of a .36 Navy Colt carved a lazy C between his vest and the front of his trousers.

"This is important." I got out the pencil stub I carried to keep track of expenses, scribbled on the back of an old hotel receipt, and handed the note of the bailiff. "Take this to him."

Reluctantly he turned and walked to the high bench and handed the fold of paper up to Blackthorne, who read it at arm's length—he apparently refused to wear his spectacles in public—and called a ten-minute recess, rapping the block with the butt of his Remington in place of a gavel. Since the day a defendant had almost gotten hold of the bailiff's Colt the Judge liked to keep the pocket gun in plain sight on the bench. While the court was still rising he strode out the side door and drew it shut behind him.

"How's Flynn?" he demanded.

I said, "He's a better man with a hole in him than a lot I could mention without. He'll likely live." I sketched out briefly the story Flynn had told me.

The Judge's brow grew as dark as his robes. "I'll not have this. Find the Mercys and tell them."

"This has to do with the Indian," I said. "Whether these are our stranglers or not, it's no coincidence they knew that was a party of lawmen. A lot of the ranchers and home-steaders in that country helped hide out Sugar Jim and his partners because they've no use for the law. Now they're helping the Indian. I want this one."

"No. You're testifying Wednesday."

"I'll head out straight from the witness chair. Another day won't make that much difference on the start the Indian has now."

"It's just your theory that he's connected with this gang. It's as full of holes as one of Colonel Hookstratton's peach tins. And your testimony may take more than one day."

"Not if I'm the first witness."

"That's up to Springer. He may have his case con-structed along entirely different lines."

"You can tell him to find new ones. I'm pulling out, with or without your leave. If without, I pull out today."

"I'll jail you for contempt of court."

"You'll have to find me first."

He said a number of things you don't often hear jurists say, unless you knew this jurist. "All right, damn you. I can't spare you and the Mercys too. Tell them they're stay-ing in Helena."

"They'll be crushed."

The Judge ignored that. "Who are you taking along?"

"The kid from Painted Rock, if he's willing. He looked pretty good standing over Sugar Jim."

"He's on his way here to testify too. But with your evidence on the stand I suppose we can make do with a signed affidavit. Springer won't like it."

"When he sees me with my suit brushed and pomade on my hair he'll be so happy it won't matter."

"Two men against an unspecified number of faceless killers isn't a hand I would bet on," he said.

"Four didn't do any too well. But you can build a fair bluff on a pair."

He ground his store-bought teeth. They sounded like china plates scraping together. "It's the Indian you want, remember. Don't go Hickoking into something that's too big for you just because Cocker Flynn's your friend."

"He's not my friend, exactly."

"Ha." He placed his hand on the doorknob. "One thing. If Jim Creel goes free because the government failed to present a strong case, you'd be wise to mail me your star."

He returned to court. I didn't tell him there was someone who could turn my star in for me.

I found Jordan Mercy holding court in the Belmont at the table where we'd had lunch, smoking what looked like another of Judge Blackthorne's long cigars and peeling out stud to his brother Joshua and Colonel Hookstratton in his tailcoat and a young miner who looked flattered to be sitting at the same table with the Mankiller of Topeka. Jordan said Jericho was occupied at Chicago Joe's. There was nothing in his manner to suggest our earlier confrontation. Nor did he display any emotion when I told him about Flynn and that his orders to leave on manhunt had been canceled. He merely nodded and flipped twenty dollars in

checks off his stack into the center of the table to open.
The young miner blanched at the amount. I left them.

I went back to my collar box of a room over the harness
shop and invested some time fully clothed on my back on
the bed, studying the water stains on the ceiling. When I
got tired of that I got up and unpegged my hat and went
down to Chicago Joe's. Jericho Mercy was coming out as
I was going in. The color on his cheeks was high.

"How was it?" I asked.

He hesitated. "The m-m-music was g-good." He kept
walking.

The place was lively. All the tables were taken and miners in overalls were lined up six deep at the bar. The dance
floor was crowded with couples shuffling their feet to the
noise from the bandstand. Jackie was there, in the arms of
a slow-faced redhead half a head taller than I. I went up
and tapped him on the shoulder. "My shift."

He was several seconds absorbing that. "Get your own.
I seen this one first."

I took out the paper twenty I had offered Duncan and
funneled it around my thumb and poked the edge against
his large nose. His eyes rolled toward the center and then
a big calloused hand came up and closed on the bill. He
peered at it closely.

"It ain't right," he said after a moment. But he let go
of Jackie and moved off. I stepped in and took his place.
Her back was stiff against my left forearm.

"That didn't look good." Her eyes, a few inches from
mine, were hard. "It looks like I'm not worth twenty dollars."

"Talk to Joe. She's the one who fixes the price. Let's
talk."

"Talking time costs the same as the other."

"That's fair." I danced her around a little. There wasn't

room to do much more than slide our feet. "Sugar Jim."
I said.

She stiffened some more. "What about him?"

"You're his favorite."

"Where'd you hear it?"

"From him."

An army of conflicting emotions marched across her face
under the heavy makeup. "He said that?" Her tone was
softer.

"Uh-huh. Men tell things to women they'd never tell
other men. Especially at certain times."

"Not to me. Not to Sugar Jim."

"He's smart. But he's still eighteen. When I was eighteen I talked about a lot of things I wouldn't talk about
now."

"What if he did? What good's it to you? He's in jail."

"His friends aren't. Harvey Byrd and the Indian."

"I don't know them," she said.

"Maybe he said some things about the places he went
to when things heated up everywhere else. Maybe the others know about those places."

The music stopped. Applause crackled. We broke apart.
Jackie's high yellow pompadour came over the brim of my
hat, but her eyes were on a level several inches below mine
and she had to look up to meet my gaze. She said, "I'm
like a doctor or a lawyer. There's things I don't tell even
if I know them. Which I'm not saying I do."

Her voice went down on the last part. We were starting
to attract attention. I lowered mine.

"You can't hurt Sugar Jim. Like you said, he's in jail."

She shook her head. "It still sounds wrong. I'll go upstairs with you if you pay, but I won't promise you anything but the usual."

"What the hell," I said, as the band started up again. I took her hand. "What the hell."

Flynn's color was better when I visited him next morning. His dark hair and moustache didn't stand out so much and someone, probably Mrs. Chrichton, had shaved off his chin stubble. He lay with those slender white hands that looked as if they belonged to someone else curled on top of the quilt and his pillow bunched behind his head. More details of that first night had come back to him. He thought that the rifle barrel that had been used to quiet the Swede belonged to a Henry, and during the exchange of gunfire he was sure he'd heard the deep hoarse roar of a Springfield. He had fought with Custer at the Washita and it was the kind of sound that stayed with you. Also the man who had given all the orders had seemed to have an accent of some kind. German, Flynn thought, but he couldn't be sure.

"A Henry, a Springfield, and a German accent," I said dryly. "How many of those can there be in Montana?"

"I'm just telling what I saw and heard." He closed his eyes. He was breathing hard from the effort of speaking. Then he opened his eyes and looked at the foot of the cot. "When you going out after the Indian?"

"Who said I was?"

He looked at me.

"Day after tomorrow, first light," I said. "I'm in court tomorrow and I'll want a fresh start." I told him about the kid from Painted Rock.

He said, "You'll need a tracker. You can't read sign for shit."

"I get by. Anyway, I talked to a friend of Sugar Jim's yesterday. There's a mining town called Teamstrike up in the Highwoods. The vein ran out and the stage stopped going there a year ago, but some die-hard prospectors are still up there cracking rock. Creel used to go there when he got unpopular other places. I'm thinking that's where we'll find Byrd and the Indian.''

"I'm thinking that's where you'll find the stranglers too.''

"It would save us some time if we did.''

"It could save you the rest of your threescore and ten.'' He shifted positions on the cot, wincing a little. "Take me along when you go.''

"You're smarter than that, Flynn. You won't even be sitting up by then.''

"I'll be standing tomorrow.''

"Over the chamber pot.''

"Go Friday. I'll be able to ride by then. Another day won't cost you if you're right about Teamstrike.''

I leaned forward in the wobbly chair I had under me. "I guess it looks like I don't have rules but I do. One of them says never ride with a man who has more than one hole in him.''

"I'm a better tracker than you.''

"Helena's full of better trackers than me. The kid knows that country. I'll go with that.''

"You'll hang with that!'' He'd started to sit up. He clamped a hand to his side and settled back, cursing breathlessly. I got up and went to the door and called for the doctor.

Chrichton came in and paused and peeled down the quilt and said,. "You've opened your dressing.''

"I noticed.'' Flynn's tone was a whisper.

"Go,'' the doctor told me. "You're as dangerous to him as that bullet.''

"I'll cut you down, Murdock, before the magpies get to you,'' said Flynn to my back. I closed the door on the rest of it.

Mrs. Chrichton was standing at the open top drawer of the big oaken file cabinet in the office. When I came in she looked up and said, "Your friend will be all right."

"Thanks," I said, fingering my hat. "I had a hunch."

Her eyelids flickered. There were cracks at the corners of her eyes, but her face didn't look as hard today. "I'm sorry for what I said yesterday. It's just that gunshot wounds make me so angry."

"Me too."

"If you men stopped wearing guns, my husband would have a lot more time to cure people who are really sick."

"You're probably right. Who would you have stop wearing them first?"

The hardness returned in two deep lines from her nostrils to her mouth. She seemed about to say something when her husband called from the back room for alcohol. She closed her mouth and slammed the file drawer shut and got a bottle out of one of the glass cabinets and walked past me and through the door. I got out of there.

I wondered if the rest of my posse had shown up yet. I stepped into the large cool carpeted velvet-hung lobby of the hotel and gave the kid's name to a clerk with a long skull and a small moustache, who glanced at the registration book on the desk and told me he had just been shown up to Eleven. I went upstairs. The kid's door was standing open and he was unpacking a scuffed brown leather valise on the bed. I rapped on the door. He looked up with a fresh shirt in one hand and a money belt in the other and his gun still in his holster slung over a corner post of the bed. He had a lot to learn.

Something just short of gladness, but a long way from hostility, crossed his face when he recognized me. He got rid of the shirt and we shook hands quickly. He had shaved off his hopeless moustache, which had the odd effect of making him look older, and my first thought was that he seemed more composed, less unsure of himself than I remembered, but then I was looking at him from this side of that flame-spiked night in camp with an experienced killer helpless at his feet. To everyone else he was probably just another twenty-year-old kid in a frontier loaded with them.

I watched him peel off the jacket and pull his shirt out of his pants and buckle the money belt around his waist under the shirt and said, "Next time you do something like that, close the door and keep your gun close. This town's full of prospectors looking for a stake."

"I reckon you're right." He looked thoughtful tucking the shirt back in over the belt. "We going to put Sugar Jim away tomorrow?"

"That's the plan."

"Pa didn't like my coming. He says I'm away too much now. But I don't much take to ranching."

"Change your mind about marshaling?"

"I don't know. You don't look to of got rich off it."

"If it's getting rich you're after," I said, "dump out that belt and invest in a mule and a pan. I hear east of the Missouri they're tripping over nuggets fit to choke a pig."

He shook his head. "Too much work."

"Want a job?"

"Depends on what you're paying." He unhooked his gun belt from the bedpost, watching me.

"Posse pay's six cents a mile, plus whatever reward Judge Blackthorne decides is right for the Indian and his partner. More if we get the men he wants most." I told him about the bunch that jumped Flynn and his party.

"Well, which are we after?"

"The Indian, so far as anyone is supposed to know. I'm thinking the others will find us soon enough." I paused. "We?"

He grinned shamefacedly, tugging the cartridge belt tight over his hips. "Six cents is six cents, I reckon."

It was my turn to shake my head. Just for a while there I'd thought he was smarter than I ever was.

TWELVE

The lawyer defending Sugar Jim Creel was named Devereaux. He was a New Orleans creole, a bull-chested man of forty with no neck and a great mane of shaggy dark hair parted in the middle and bulging out and down like a haystack almost to his shoulders, built from the waist up to be six-two but teetering on bent, shriveled legs that chopped him off around five-five. His hands swung at knee level when he paced the rectangle of varnished floor between the bench and the gallery, making him look from the back like a gorilla in a claw-hammer coat and gray tweed trousers and spats. From the front he looked like Oscar Wilde. The Creel case was his debut in Judge Blackthorne's court, but it would not be his last appearance. In years to come he would become the first attorney to win a reversal of a Blackthorne ruling in the United States Supreme Court, run unsuccessfully for the first governorship of the state of Montana, and serve as adviser on Western affairs to President Woodrow Wilson before dying in Washington City of a heart attack at the age of seventy-four in the company of a woman of doubtful fame. His family had fled France during the Terror, taking with them enough gold and jewels to reconstruct Louisiana along lines pleasing to them and purchase an education for their most promising descendant in the finest law school in the East.

That alone was enough to arouse Blackthorne's distrust. Devereaux's aggressive methods didn't improve the relationship. From the start, the course of the Creel trial was a broken string of objections from the prosecution and stern warnings from the bench to the defense counsel, the record striped with scratchovers where Blackthorne had ordered this remark or that line of questioning stricken. To someone listening outside the courtroom the Judge's harsh, clipped syllables and the lawyer's slurring, insinuating bass must have sounded like the growling of two strange dogs marking out their territories. The cartoonist from the Helena paper picked up on that image and delighted in drawing their profiles leaning muzzle to muzzle over the bench, the Judge's a snarling terrier's, Devereaux's large and calm and quietly menacing like a sheepdog's. The Judge had the artist banned from his court after that. Devereaux had one of the cartoons framed and hung over his desk.

I still have the trial transcript. It was given to me a few years ago by someone who rescued it from the trash bin behind the courthouse after the committee appointed by the president to reorganize the court after Blackthorne's death ordered everything thrown out that they might begin again with nothing to remind them of the unpleasant past. Here is a piece of my testimony under cross-examination, with the scratched-out parts restored from memory.

DEVEREAUX: What was your responsibility in the party pursuing Mr. Creel?

MURDOCK: I was in charge.

DEVEREAUX: And the men under you? What were their responsibilities?

MURDOCK: Dad Miller and Charley Rudabaugh were officers like me, deputized by the United States Federal Court at Helena with jurisdiction over Montana Territory. We picked up the kid at Painted Rock because he knew the country, and the Indian, Virgil Blue Water, was our tracker.

DEVEREAUX: Is it not true that each member of a posse is chosen for his special—shall we say, talents?

SPRINGER: Objection. Your honor, I fail to see the relevance of this line of questioning.

DEVEREAUX: If the court will bear with me a few moments, I hope to establish relevance.

BLACKTHORNE: Very well, counselor. But do not be all day about it.

DEVEREAUX: Shall I repeat the question, Deputy Murdock?

MURDOCK: No. Yes, it is customary before going on a manhunt to stack your deck.

DEVEREAUX: Meaning that every man in the party is a specialist of some sort.

MURDOCK: Yes.

DEVEREAUX: What was Deputy Rudabaugh's specialty?

MURDOCK: He was a good shot.

DEVEREAUX: Surely that is not unique? Were you not all good shots?

MURDOCK: Some of us were better than others.

DEVEREAUX: Come now, Deputy. We are all adults. What, precisely, made Rudabaugh so valuable to your mission?

MURDOCK: I had worked with him before and found him to be a reliable man.

DEVEREAUX: I happen to know that you turned down two officers for that third spot, both men with whom you had worked before and to good success. Every man in that party had something the others did not. Dad Miller had the most experience. You had leadership ability. Virgil Blue Water could track and the other young man was familiar with the area. What appealed to you about Rudabaugh?—Your honor, I request that the court direct the witness to answer my question.

BLACKTHORNE: The witness is so directed.

MURDOCK: Rudabaugh had the fastest reflexes of all of us and I could expect him to put a bullet where it would do the most good when it would do us the most good to have it there.

DEVEREAUX: Was Charlie Rudabaugh in fact a hired assassin?

SPRINGER: Your honor, I object to this shabby attempt on the part of the defense to impugn the integrity of this witness.

DEVEREAUX: Had he integrity to impugn, I might withdraw the question.

BLACKTHORNE: I will have none of these sly asides, counselor. Objection sustained. The jury will disregard and the recorder will strike everything after the witness's last statement. Rephrase your question, Mr. Devereaux.

DEVEREAUX: Is it not true, Deputy Murdock, that Charley Rudabaugh's chief responsibility while he was riding with you was to kill on command?

SPRINGER: Objection.

MURDOCK: No, I will answer the question. Yes, I chose him because his hand would not be slowed like yours or mine by Christian principles. It is a wild country up there, and when you are on a manhunt you must regard everyone you meet as an enemy until you learn otherwise. The benefit of the doubt lends too much advantage to the other side.

DEVEREAUX: You shock me, Deputy. What, then, is there to separate you from those you have been deputized to protect us from?

MURDOCK: Sometimes it is just our badges.

BLACKTHORNE: I will have order here.

DEVEREAUX: I must say that I fail to see what can be gained by riding with men no better than the men you pursue.

MURDOCK: You might if you ever found yourself looking down the ugly end of Sugar Jim's forty-four.

BLACKTHORNE: Order.

DEVEREAUX: Are you trying to be clever, Deputy Murdock?

MURDOCK: Sorry. I did not mean to get ahead of you.

It's all there, or most of it anyhow, written on long sheets of paper going brown and cracking apart like mummy wrappings. But the words alone don't say anything about the angry red of Prosecutor Springer's countenance above his whiskers when he rose to object or Devereaux's mugging for the jury or the noise from the gallery or Sugar Jim sitting behind the defense table in a clean shirt buttoned to the neck with his hair plastered down and his hands folded in front of him like a boy half his age taking an arithmetic lesson. At this point the Judge called the noon recess early to let things calm down. When court reconvened an hour and a half later, the defense attorney reported that he was through with his cross-examination, after which Springer redirected a few questions to dispel the clouds Devereaux had managed to raise over my testimony and to tamp down its main points. Then I was dismissed and the clerk called the kid from Painted Rock for Devereaux to challenge his affidavit, which had been read into the record that morning.

"How are we doing?" I whispered to Springer at the prosecution table.

"That's what someone asked Custer." He glowered in his beard.

I think the kid surprised Devereaux. On the stand he uncorked the same tense control he had demonstrated the night we were jumped, answering the lawyer's leading questions promptly, neither contradicting his earlier statements nor allowing himself to be drawn into a corner. Invited by the Judge to redirect, a pleased Springer replied that he had no questions for the witness. The kid stepped down. Blackthorne adjourned for the day.

"We broke even," announced the prosecutor, rocking on his heels in the hall outside the main doors with his hands in his pockets. The kid and I were with him. "We may or may not be able to nail him on the ambush. But we've laid a fair foundation for the case for the surveyor's murder. This may work out better than I'd planned. I had intended originally to lead off with that and then go on to the other charges."

"If you don't get him for the ambush," I said, "what's that do for the case against the Indian and Byrd?"

"It will weaken it. Neither of you actually saw them during the shooting, and if the government fails to establish Creel's guilt it will be difficult to convict them on the basis of their friendship with the accused." He nodded to each of us and left, towering over the last spectators to leave the courtroom loitering in the hallway.

"All broke up," remarked the kid.

I said, "I guess he figures once is enough to hang a man. His job doesn't start until we've done ours."

"Kind of makes you see why folks take up lynching."

I put on my hat. "Trouble is this bunch is wasting its rope on the wrong part of the law. Let's get supper."

"Belmont?"

"No, I'm getting not to like the crowd they're attracting. Let's go to the hotel."

Things weren't much better there. Colonel Hookstratton and Frank Willard were sharing a table and a chicken in the hotel dining room, the Colonel sweetening his coffee from a steel pocket flask. I told the kid to get us a table and paused beside theirs.

"I kind of thought you two and the Chief would be moving on after Sunday," I said.

"We had such plans." Hookstratton corked the flask and returned it to the inside pocket of his tailcoat. "However, I have accepted an assignment from the Omaha *Herald* to cover Sugar Jim's trial. Perhaps you saw me there."

"You're not easy to miss." He had taken up at least three places in the gallery.

"Your Judge Blackthorne has denied me an interview with the defendant. I am considering appealing his decision to the territorial governor."

"Don't bother. He answers only to Congress and the president. By the time you get the wire back from Washington City the trial will be over and Sugar Jim will be kicking clouds out from under his feet."

"You seem certain he will be convicted and hanged."

"Is that for you or the Omaha *Herald*?" I asked.

His white handlebars twisted. "I will say 'Deputies declined to speculate on Creel's fate.' " He sipped his coffee. "In addition, Marshal Mercy's response to my overtures to meet with him and his brothers for the purpose of a new book was encouraging. I think of titling it *The Three Mercys of Helena*. It has rather a biblical ring, do you not agree?"

"What have they done here worth writing about?"

He swallowed some more coffee and picked up his fork. "Well, I shall not talk myself dry of things best said in print. I think your friend wants your attention."

The kid was sitting at an empty table a dozen feet away. He had a menu in his hand and a bald waiter with a strawberry mark on his face was standing over him. "Waiter says the trout's fresh," the kid called.

"Fresh from the salt barrel. Order chicken." I looked at the Colonel. "They're generous in Omaha, to pay your way and the Chief's and Willard's too."

"Belly kills his own meals and sleeps in the open. And Frank has secured temporary employment."

Willard's hot eyes fixed me over the drumstick he was gnawing. "I'm working for the Mercys," he said through a mouthful of bird.

"Doing what?"

"Things and things," supplied Hookstratton, and toasted

me with his cup. "Enjoy your meal, Deputy. You have made an excellent choice in the chicken."

I went to my table and ate supper with the kid. That was my last night in Helena for a while.

THIRTEEN

Smeary blue light spread five perfect fingers against the black sky in the east, icing the broken-bottle peaks of the Big Belts as we swung around the west end of town and turned north. I was on the sorrel and the kid rode a leggy three-year-old bay stallion bearing his father's brand. We had no pack animal, just one canteen apiece and what dried meat and corn we could get into our saddlebags. We would be touching civilization once or twice before Team-strike. The air was cool in the before-dawn, but the dew on the grass wasn't frozen and you had to look to see your breath. Spring comes late to Montana but when it comes it stays.

We hadn't said a word to each other since meeting in front of the livery, and crossing the oil black Missouri and starting the long, easy climb to the foothills we still kept silent. That augured well for the rest of our time together; I didn't trust men who talked much before sunup. On the Sugar Jim run, the Indian's mouth had generally started flapping the minute he got out from under his blanket and kept on until he ran out of things to say. You can hide a lot under a wordslide. Ahead of us, that broken-off piece of the Continental Divide looked like lumped blue ice as we climbed, steam rolling off the horses' withers now, and then suddenly a pie-shaped wedge of sun as bright as a powder flash appeared from behind the rocks and struck a long white spark off a glistening edge.

"Jesus!" Temporarily blinded, the kid wrestled his whistling bay's forefeet back down to earth.

"That's the thing you have to look for at first light in the mountains," I said, when he had the horse under control.

"I don't usually hit 'em going east." He looked questioningly at the sorrel, which was as calm as a toad on a warm rock.

I said, "He's used to it. Also gelding takes the yellow out of them."

"I always thought that went the other way."

"Once you've had that done there's not much else that can scare you."

"I'll take the being scared," said the kid.

We turned our shoulders to the sun until it was high and out of the way, taking our time and sparing the horses on the long grade. The hills were going rich green under last year's dead brown coat. Droplets of condensed moisture winked in the sun and lifted to form a thick layer like spun silver and then burned off. The grass dried and straightened. The air warmed. After noon we stripped off our jackets and stashed them behind our cantles and didn't put them on again until the sun was sucking down orange and purple streamers in the west.

At that point we had an hour's light and a good moon, but since we were near the kid's home we turned that way. A rider intercepted us. It was the kid's father.

He was a fair picture of what his son would look like in thirty years, thicker in the arms and torso but just as long, with a flinty gray moustache that chased his jowls and lines so deep in his burned face they resembled the decorative scars that the Indians of some tribes gave each other to prove how little they were bothered by pain. He wore his hat brim funneled down in front past the bridge of his nose and a canvas coat and jeans and a Dragoon pistol in a holster turned behind his hip bone. He wasn't any happier to see me than he had been the last time I'd borrowed his son, but he agreed to put us up in the house for the night. We accompanied him to the barn and turned our horses over to a bearded stable hand.

Ranch headquarters was a long log building with inside window shutters fixed with gunports left over from the days when the Sioux and Shoshone and northern Cheyenne still claimed the land. We ate stew served by the rancher's wife—his second, the kid had told me, and just two years older than his son—and while we were eating I casually brought up the subject of stranglers.

"It's a day's ride to law from here," said the old man, smearing butter over a slice of hot bread. "I wore the bark off a limb or two in the bad times, when horse thieves was thick as grubs on a wet log. I ain't saying I wouldn't again if I thought there wasn't justice in Helena. But that fellow Blackthorne don't shy from the rope. He's got my vote for governor if we ever get to be a state, God curse the day."

"The stranglers I'm interested in don't hang horse thieves," I said. "They've been stringing up law."

He ate the bread without changing expression. "This have to do with them two you and the boy found swinging up north?"

"As like as not. Maybe you heard something."

"The boy tell you I did?"

"No," said the kid, looking at him.

The rancher used the rest of his bread to mop up the gravy from his plate. "My closest neighbor's a day off and

I can't spare the day, being short one hand most of the time." He didn't look at his son. He didn't have to. "I don't hear much new till it's old."

I nodded, eating. "Well, I'd be just as happy if not everyone knew we'd been here asking about stranglers."

"I got better things to do than spread gossip. Being short one hand like I am." He called to his wife for coffee.

After supper the kid and I went to the barn to look to the horses. The kid said, "I don't know if that's the straight of it, what Pa said about not hearing nothing. I ain't around enough to know what folks is talking about."

I fired up a lantern and inspected each of the sorrel's shoes for loose nails. The kid kept talking.

"That was a mistake, asking Pa not to tell no one what we're about. He's got better things to do than spread gossip, but he spreads it anyway."

"That's what I count on." I handed the lantern to the kid, whose face screwed up for a moment in its molten light, then smoothed into something close to a smile. He bent to see to his bay's shoes.

We spent the night on feather mattresses, likely to be our last for a while, and set out again at dawn with a hot breakfast in our bellies and not so much as a good-bye from the kid's father. "He ain't long on warm," said the kid.

"That burns out soon up here," I told him.

Half an hour out we came upon the remains of Cocker Flynn's camp, the scene of the ambush. It had rained hard there recently, but the bank of rocks the deputies had started to set up for a fire that was never kindled and the mangled grass and earth where the frightened horses had plunged and wheeled during the shooting identified the spot. Here and there were brown patches darker than the bare earth, patches the rain hadn't quite been able to wash away and wouldn't for a long time. Nothing stains deeper than blood.

After a search we picked up a faint trail left by a fair number of horses and followed it to the Smith River, where we lost it. The kid crossed over and we picked our way in both directions along the squirming banks for two miles, studying the ground. We met back where we'd started.

The kid said, "Seems a long way to walk a stream bed this time of year."

"Not if you want to shake law off your spurs." We gave it up and went on to Great Falls.

The settlement was named for the roaring, steaming cataract in that knotted section of the Missouri, but it wouldn't find its way onto the maps for another two years, when the gold and silver prospectors that made up most of its population accidentally stumbled on copper, and then the smelters came in and attracted refining business from Helena and Butte. Some called the place Drewyer's Shot for the member of Lewis and Clark's party who had thus extricated himself from a situation there involving a tree and a fifteen-hundred-pound grizzly. The collection of log buildings stood on the edge of a hundred miles of trees clustered so thickly that in full leaf they looked from the mountains like an enormous lush pasture.

We attracted some attention riding down a street of ropy mud fetlock-deep. The place didn't get that many visitors, and stubble-faced men in faded flannel shirts and thready overalls swept balding buffalo robes and tattered blankets aside from the doorways to look out and see who was coming in to beat them out of their prospective claims. Many of them held big brown-barreled rifles.

None of the buildings was marked, but from my last visit I remembered which belonged to the sheriff and we dismounted and tied up in front of it. I knocked mud off my boots and led the way inside.

It was more house than office, furnished with a minimum

of chairs and a crate bed with a straw mattress and a bear rug on the earth floor and a stove fashioned from a piece of locomotive boiler plate, its bent pipe escaping through a missing window pane, a greasy rag stuffed around it. A man with his hair combed forward over his scalp and a ring of dark beard like a coal-smear around his mouth was sitting at a rough table that did for a desk near the back wall. He was wearing overalls and looked like just another prospector, which he was, part-time. This was the sheriff of Great Falls. He had a shotgun cut back to pistol length pointed at our bellies.

"Throw up your hands, boys," he said quietly, in a voice webby with phlegm.

We obeyed. I said, "Page Murdock, Sheriff. We met when I came through with Sugar Jim. You remember the kid."

"Yeah." The shotgun didn't move. "I remember. You borrowed two of my best men. They're waiting for you at the saloon."

"They're all right?" asked the kid, astonished.

I told him to keep his mouth shut.

The sheriff stood. He was skinny but had a round belly like a snake digesting a hen's egg whole. "They're waiting. Let's go see them. I didn't say you could drop your hands."

The last part came out harsh. Still holding the shotgun, he told us to turn around and he came forward and lifted our guns out of our holsters and patted our chests and boots onehanded for hideouts. He straightened. "All right, hands down. Out that door and to your right, two doors down."

We walked along a rough plank that served as a boardwalk with him behind us carrying the shotgun under the close attention of the other men on the street and turned and went through the empty doorway he'd directed us to. The room was dim and stank heavily of beer and spitoons.

There were no tables in the saloon, just a bar made from another plank laid across two barrels with two more men in overalls leaning on it, watching us with glasses in their hands, and a man who was all tangled dark beard and sunken eyes and huge forearms filling a bottle from a horizontal barrel behind it. The sheriff caught his eye and he nodded once and the shotgun pushed the base of my spine and we went around the bar and through another door. That led to a back room that was actually a lean-to, containing more barrels and stacked firewood, on top of which lay an old and a young body feet to feet.

Their necks were as long as a neck could get, short of decapitation.

The kid's nostrils went white, but aside from that he showed no reaction. He had seen and done a thing or two since his first sight of hanged men. I said, "Where's the Swede?"

"If you mean that other one," said the sheriff, "we buried him where we found them. He had a hole in his chest and a cracked skull to go with the stretched neck. These two have friends here and relatives back East that might want to come read their markers someday. We didn't have horse enough to carry all three."

His mouth didn't open any wider than the shotgun muzzle to let out the words. I asked where he'd found the slain deputies.

"Just this side of the Shonkin Sag. There's trees enough to go around there."

"That's Highwood Mountain country," said the kid.

The sheriff nodded, watching me. "This Swede fellow a friend of yours?"

"He was a deputy U.S. marshal."

"He wasn't wearing no star."

"Some killers take what they figure is handy," I said.

He considered. Then he lowered the shotgun and took a loud breath. "I reckon we're all of us losers here."

"Maybe you more than us." I accepted the return of our guns and handed the kid his Colt.

"Old Chubb Bowles there was a good lawman and a better partner." Suddenly the sheriff snorted. "Once he thought we struck the lode and rode all the way to Helena for French champagne. Didn't blink an eye when he got back and found out the gold was iron sulfide. Just knocked the necks off all the bottles and passed them around."

"Funny what being dead will do for you," I said. "I found him sour."

"That was just his way till he knew you. Town wanted him for sheriff on account of he used to be a ranger, but he said I was a better organizer and took deputy instead. That was just smoke. He knew I had a bad back and that way I could sit in the office while he done the digging and we'd still be partners." He breathed some more air. "Reckon now I got to dig *and* sheriff."

"Any idea which way the lynchers took?"

He shook his head. "It's mostly rock there, and we had a real gully washer night before last. If they left tracks at all they was gone hours before we got there."

"Who's *we*?" I pressed.

"Me and three other miners. Dutch Ike was working out that way and come back to say he found Chubb and young Tim there twisting, plus the other one."

"These other miners deputies?"

"More or less. You'll find no badges here, but hunting for gold you go a little crazy sometimes and somebody's got to keep these fellows from bashing each other's heads in."

I said, "I'd like to borrow one or two for a few days. They'll get posse pay and maybe a piece of a reward."

"For the ones that lynched Chubb and Tim?"

"Just now we're looking for someone else."

"Looking in which direction?" he asked.

"Teamstrike."

"Can't help you." He checked the abbreviated shotgun to make sure the hammer was down and slid it under his belt.

"Why not?"

"I'm just here to keep my friends from turning killer, like I said. I don't get a badge nor pay except two cents for every rat and stray dog I shoot in the vicinity and three squares a day here at the saloon. For that I don't go to no places like Teamstrike. You can talk to the others but they'll tell you the same."

"It's just a miner's town like this one," put in the kid.

The sheriff spat. "No such a thing. Maybe it started out that way, but just now it's a place to stop for all the scum in the territory on their way to Canada. Coffee's six dollars a pound there on account of them that buy it dassn't show their faces in any right town. They'd smell law coming for two miles and shoot it from one. I'd sooner overnight in hell."

He paused to measure out a long look for each of us. "If that's where you two are fixing to go," he said, "don't look for us to come in and dig you a hole."

FOURTEEN

"How many you figure?" I drew my sleeve across my mouth and corked my canteen.

The kid had just rejoined me after trotting his horse to a high mound and standing in his stirrups for the best part of five minutes, looking west. At my question he raised his eyebrows.

"You knew we were being followed?" he asked.

I slung the canteen over my saddle horn. "Ever since Great Falls. I spotted him before that, but I thought he was just a prospector. See any more than just the one?"

He shook his head. "He's riding a gray. Time to time he steps off and looks at the ground. Once he looked straight up at me, but I don't think he seen nothing. Looking down's easier than looking up, especially at this distance."

We were coming up the north slope of the Highwoods, with the ground angling sharply off behind us and the trees to our right catching fire in the lowering sun. Shadows blended the young pines in the sunken hammock of the Shonkin Sag at our backs into a dark even green like the felt on a billiard table. The channel had been carved during the last Ice Age by the stubborn Missouri when a glacier got in its way. The air up there was colder, swifter, thinner, and I could feel my cheeks and chin going numb in the wind.

We'd be sleeping with our canteens that night to keep them from icing up.

"What do we do?" asked the kid.

"About what?"

He bristled. "About our friend back there, that's about what."

"What would you suggest?"

"Well, you're the law."

"That looks like a level spot east a ways," I said, pointing with the peak of my hat brim. "We'll camp there tonight."

"And just let him come up on us while we're sleeping?"

"*We* don't sleep. You sleep and then I sleep. If he's one of our stranglers I can't think of a better way to make his acquaintance. But he won't be coming up here tonight."

"I'd admire to know why," he said patiently.

"Those white things you see getting in the way of the sky are called clouds. He won't have a moon to read signs by, and if he's dumb enough to try this grade in the dark he's nothing we have to worry about."

"If he was in Great Falls he knows where we're headed."

"If he felt safe enough to talk to the sheriff," I agreed. "But just like us he's got this mountain between him and Teamstrike."

"If I had a Sharps or even a Springfield I could pick him off clean from here."

I didn't say anything to that. The kid was too easy.

The level area was carpeted with sweet shoots of grass. We saved our corn by letting the horses graze and built a small fire behind a thick stand of firs for a break. The wind moaned up in the peaks and spiraled down to shiver the trees, bringing with it the metallic odor of snow that never melted. We wound ourselves in our blankets to the ears and tipped our hats forward and sat down and chewed dried meat as tough as birch bark and watched the coffee come to a boil on a flat rock next to the flames.

"You always been a deputy?" asked the kid.

"That's a damn fool question," I said. "You always been twenty?"

"I'm twenty-one. I mean, what did you do before?"

"I punched cows. Before that I punched more cows and before that I punched some more and before that I shot Rebel snipers out of trees. Between times I collected bedsores in an army hospital watching the bones in my leg knit. Anything else?"

"Just asking," he said. "I bet you was born out here. I can always spot them."

"You'd lose."

"Grew up here, then."

I nodded. "In a little town you never heard of up in the Bitterroots. It's gone now. The beaver trapped out finally and wolves came in and ate the cattle. You might find a board lying around there if you looked hard."

We didn't talk again for a space. I wrapped my kerchief around one hand and plucked the smoking coffee pot up by its handle and filled our tin cups and set the pot down a little farther away from the fire and handed the kid his cup and warmed my hands around mine.

"What you figure's waiting for us in Teamstrike?" The kid blew steam off his cup.

"Mean looks, mostly. That kind generally won't bring more trouble on themselves than they've got to start with. Unless we do more than stop to buy a beer on our way through. Which is just what we're fixing to do, if the Indian is there.''

"You really want the Indian, huh?"

"No more than I want the ones that shot Flynn and killed the Swede," I said.

"Well, sure, Flynn's your friend and the Swede was one of your own. But you got a thing about the Indian."

"Maybe."

"He done the same thing, though."

"No, the Indian turned."

He said, "How's that worse?"

"I don't know that it's worse." The coffee scalded my tongue. I set the cup aside to cool in the shadows beyond the firelight. "My father had a retriever, all gold with a white star on its chest. A neighbor came to visit one day when the dog and my father were in front of the house and the dog up and bit him. My father went inside and got his shotgun and loaded both barrels and came back out and blew the dog's brains apart. The neighbor said, 'Why'd you have to go and do that, Edan? It wasn't much of a bite and the dog was a good hunter.' 'Next time,' my father said, 'he might have bitten me.' "

The fire burned down to its red core. Somewhere in the darkness wings fluttered with a noise like a locomotive going wide open and something squealed and the wings beat away.

The kid said, "I never shot anyone."

"You start by watching his hands."

"I heard it was eyes."

"Eyes don't kill," I said. "Watch his hands and say to yourself you're going to kill him. Hoping it won't come to that will just slow you down and then he'll kill you. It's got nothing to do with being faster or a better shot. There's no skill to it at all. Anyone can do it."

"Sounds hard to me."

"It is. The first five times."

We finished our coffee and I laid some more wood on the fire and got up to take the first watch.

Nothing happened that night. In the dawn gray we reheated the pot and I got out the black iron skillet and greased it with bacon drippings from the can I carried in my saddlebags and paved the skillet with strips of dehydrated beef. At first the stuff coiled and twisted like surprised scorpions, but as the hot grease soaked in, the meat swelled and softened. The smell in the cold early-morning air on a wooded mountain was stomach-scraping.

"Page," said the kid.

It was the first time he'd addressed me by my Christian name. Turning the meat over in the pan with a fork, I asked him what he wanted. When he didn't reply I looked up. He was crouched on the other side of the fire with his eyes trained past my left shoulder.

I was squatting on my heels. I dropped the fork and pivoted on my right foot, throwing myself backward onto my hams as I swept the Deane-Adams out of its holster. Something metallic crunched, and suddenly the rest of my life was no longer than the barrel of a big cocked Colt staring me in the face.

"I've known warmer welcomes," said a familiar voice on the other side of the gun.

He'd maneuvered to have the sun behind him, and in the shadow of his Stetson his black bar of brow and gracefully curving moustache blended into the vague dark outline of his face, but there was no disguising that voice, flat as a piece of shale slapping the surface of a pond, or the short square solid build under the drab sturdy clothes. I said, "I gave you credit for having more brains than to pick your way up a mountain with no moon, Flynn. Or did you leave them behind at the Smith River?''

''I used your fire for a mark and moved slow on foot. You can do it when time's on your neck.''

I introduced the kid to Cocker Flynn without taking my eyes or my gun off the newcomer. Neither of them spoke to the other. Flynn's gun was equally motionless. We'd both been lawmen too long to be the first to surrender the point.

We might have gone on like that all day had not Flynn begun to sway and the Colt to wobble. I reached up and grasped his wrist in my free hand, pushing the weapon to one side while getting my feet under me to support him. I let down the hammer on the English revolver and he did the same and we leathered the guns. I got Flynn to sit down on my blanket. He took off his hat. In that cold there was a skin of perspiration over the pulpy gray of his face.

I handed him my flask. He had trouble getting the cork out, but when he tipped up the container his hand was steady. A slow flush dyed his cheeks.

''How'd you get away from Doc Chrichton?'' I demanded.

''He was out making rounds and his wife left to see to somebody pregnant. She thought I was asleep. Mind my horse don't wander off while I'm telling you history,'' he told the kid.

The kid looked at me. I nodded and he struck off toward the firs in the direction Flynn had indicated. We heard him making kissing noises to avoid panicking the animal. I said, ''Let's see your wounds.''

The older deputy let me open his coat and pull up his shirt and peel away the bandages from the entry and exit holes in his side. The stitches were leaking, but they had held. "There's extra dressing in my saddlebags," he said with a grunt. "I grabbed a double handful on my way through the office. Also laudanum, but I couldn't find but one little bottle, and that half gone. Drank the last of that last night."

When the kid led Flynn's big gray, blowing and crusted with frozen lather, into camp, I had him get out the dressing and washed both wounds from the flask and rebandaged them. Meanwhile the kid knocked ice off the exhausted horse and threw the saddle and bridle and rubbed the animal down with its blanket from muzzle to tail. Flynn said, "We're burning daylight."

"We'll burn a lot more before we pull out," I said. "You can kill yourself if you like, but your horse is worth something."

The meat had burned to old black lace in the skillet. I scraped it out with my knife and greased it again and cooked some more strips and we ate them and washed them down with whiskey-seasoned coffee. Afterward Flynn's color was almost normal.

"I stopped at my place for fresh clothes and feed and some tinned goods, but a man needs meat," he said gratefully, sucking bacon grease off his fingers. "Picked up your trail where they hit me and the Swede and the rest. I knew where you was going, but there ain't no telling how many holes two young fools like you can drop into on the way."

Flynn had just three years on me, but I let him play the old scout. I asked him if he'd stopped in Great Falls.

"No time. I come around it and picked you up again this side. I've had more trouble trailing buffalo by the herd."

"Law don't need to cover its tracks," said the kid.

Flynn gave him one of his flat looks, then turned it on

me. I ignored it and told him what we'd found in town and what the sheriff had told us. He listened, producing a flat tin of tobacco from a pocket and placing a pinch of the sodden black stuff between his lower lip and his gum. The slight bulge reinforced his natural truculent look. He'd liked the Swede.

"Outlaw town's a bad thing," he said. "They'll kill you soon as shake your hand them places. How you figure to get in?"

I said, "Front door."

"Day or night?"

"Day. People look harder at you by dark."

"The Indian knows both of you," he said. "Clank one shoe down in town and if he's there he'll sing out."

"I'd welcome a better plan."

"The Indian don't know me. I'll go in and see is he there and report back. Just like we done it at the Washita."

"You were doing fine right up until you rang in Custer," I said.

He let that pass. "I'm thinking night. Maybe they look harder at you then, but they don't see as much."

The kid said, "You can't hardly stand, let alone ride into a town full of killers."

"Son, I eat bullets and sweat dead Indians. There ain't a horse I can't saddle nor a man I can't beat in a fair fight. When Shoshone was thick here they called me Wolf Runner on account I used to run down wolves afoot and snap their necks with my bare hands for fun. I go through women like a dose of salts and whiskey like it was water and my head's so hard my pa never owned an anvil. Remember what I look like so you can tell your grandkids, because you'll not see another man like me if you get to be a hundred."

Winded a little from the speech, Flynn spat black juice and spat back against my saddle, drawing from the flask. The kid looked at me for a translation.

I grinned. "He said he's going into Teamstrike."

FIFTEEN

Cocker Flynn slept until almost noon in the shade of the mountain while his horse grazed and rested and the kid and I cleaned weapons that didn't need cleaning. Things stirred in the warming air. A squirrel scolded us from the top of a sixty-foot pine and a thousand feet above that an eagle hung in a sky stained slightly with clouds, wary of the men and horses down below that weren't up and moving in the middle of the day. Except for the squirrel it was quiet enough there to make a man think he could hear the muted roar of the Missouri falls ten miles to the west.

Flynn rose stiffly without being roused and we saddled up and followed an old glacier scar up and around the shoulder of the mountain, leading the horses over the loose treacherous surface of rockfalls with grass and jack pines growing dementedly between them. The older lawman used a rock to smash the head of a rattlesnake that had startled his gray from its sunning place atop a granite outcrop.

"That for you, Indian," Flynn muttered.

A mile in that country was worth five on the level. We stopped often to blow the horses while Flynn rested and the kid and I plucked burrs off our clothes and shook pebbles out of our boots. Flynn was always the first up, never mind how his color came and went.

"Wolf Runner," snarled the kid, picking up his bay's reins.

We came around the mountain and looked down on Teamstrike. A clutter of log huts and board shacks caught in the valley cleft like trash in a drained basin; the town drew its water from springs that turned the passages between buildings—you could hardly call them streets—into slimy blue clay that made Great Falls seem dry by comparison. Greasy brown light slid out through windows of clouded glass and oiled paper, and in the still of sunset a piano splattered broken notes up to our perch. Horses stood switching their tails in corrals built of crooked tree limbs with the bark still on.

"Ugly's too good a word for it," said Flynn.

"The Indians considered this place sacred," the kid informed us. "They called it the Valley of Beautiful Dreams."

Flynn spat. "Well, it's sure enough a nightmare now."

We waited while the sun eased itself down behind the range like an old man sinking into a scalding tub. Then Flynn took his horse by the bit and started forward. After two steps he stopped and unpinned his star from his shirt and turned and flipped it to me. "You don't see me by midnight, bury that."

He made his way down the steep grade sideways to avoid losing his footing, the gray snorting and backing and fighting the bit but giving ground finally. The kid and I watched them moving in and out of stripes of shadow until there were no spaces between.

"Reckon he knows what he's about?" asked the kid.

"He taught me."

The night air wasn't as cold there on the lee side of the

mountain. We picketed the horses to keep them close and fed them by hand from the corn in our saddlebags and chewed dried meat cold, chasing it with water from the canteens. In the dark, the town at the base of the long slope looked almost pleasant, like lighted windows hanging in the night as seen from a moving train, and the rise and fall of voices vaguely human and piano noise couched a promise, however false, of welcome. You didn't want to go down and be part of it, but you felt as if you could spend the rest of your life sitting on the side of that mountain just looking and listening. They tell me there are hunting things on the floor of the ocean that make their victims feel just that way.

We set up hour watches. The kid stood the first while I slept. I relieved him, and shortly before my time was up something kicked a stone loose on the grade below. Bouncing down it made a noise like Judge Blackthorne's pistol butt rapping the bench for silence. I got out the Deane-Adams and rolled back the hammer.

"Murdock, don't you like me?"

It was Flynn's voice, coming up from the darkness below. I asked him if he was alone.

"Hell, no. I got my horse with me."

I uncocked and holstered the five-shot. There were some scraping noises and a shuddery snort from the horse, and then man and animal moved into the gray ice light shed by the moon through a webwork of clouds, Flynn leading the big gray. He was breathing heavily from the effort of climbing.

I woke the kid and we tethered the horse to a stunted jack pine. Flynn spoke, using the last of the whiskey in the flask.

"The town ain't all desperadoes, just more than most, like every other outlaw town I ever heard tell of," he said.

"Mostly it's prospectors and them that go wherever there's prospecting done. Two saloons with gambling and a whorehouse and a general merchandise selling eggs at a dollar a shell, swear to God, and them with good layers out back, so it ain't as if they got to pack them in over the mountains. Boardinghouse is run by a board fence in a brown dress calls herself Aunt Aurola. There's a corral back of it with a piebald in it looks mighty like the one you said the Indian was riding."

I jumped on that. "Is he staying there?"

He handed me his blank look. "Yes, I walked right up and asked Aunt Aurola was Mr. Virgil Blue Water in residence and if he was would he mind coming out so's I can arrest him for the murder of two federal deputies. How long's it been since you visited a wrong town?"

"All right. What else did you find out?"

"I done some drinking in both saloons and let the bartenders think I was on my way north and wouldn't mind if I put the border twixt me and some others in a blue-tick hurry. I listened to some talk, which there's nothing more boring when it's between men on the scout, done some walking around and talked to the boardinghouse woman and gave her five dollars to hold a bed for me whilst I seen to some business. Then I mounted up and looked over the in and out of town. Quickest way out's a pass that winds north around this mountain, I'm thinking it connects up with the Sag. We'd of saved climbing time, we knew that coming in." He looked at the kid.

"There's a rockslide blocking that pass," the kid said, "or there was last time I was in it, three years ago."

"It looks to of been blasted out for near a mile, which is as far as I followed it."

"We'll be getting out fast," I said. "We won't want any nasty surprises like a mountain standing in front of us."

The kid said, "Maybe we ought to check it out by day-light."

Flynn shook his head and squirted tobacco. "There'll be prospectors crawling all over then. And I can't say how long my story will stand up."

"Lay out the boardinghouse for me," I told him.

"There's a front door opens on the rest of town and a back leading into the corral. Two floors, with outside stairs going up to the second. I don't know how many rooms."

"Windows?"

"Four. Two in front, one on top of the other, and one each side, second floor. None in back. That's the side catches the wind through the pass. It's the last building but one on the middle path, facing south."

I said, "If it's an all-night town it starts to get quiet an hour before sunup. We won't want to run into the Indian by accident on the street with friends, so let's move then, go in the back where we won't be seen from a window."

"Likely the door will be bolted," Flynn pointed out.

"No, it won't."

He watched my face in the moonlight for a moment. Then he nodded. "I reckon it'd be a shame to waste that five dollars."

"Be at the back door when it starts to get light," I said. "If the Indian's there I want you to tell me what room he's in, and Harvey Byrd too if he's there."

"You want breakfast while I'm at it?"

"Only if it's hot." I cuffed him lightly on the shoulder. "You didn't happen to see your friend with the Mexican spurs."

"I think I'd of said that first if I did." He handed me the empty flask. "Reckon I'll go remind myself what it feels like to have feathers under me. You young fellows be sure and shake out your blankets for snakes." He picked

up the gray's reins again and led it away toward the lights
of town.

After that the kid and I traded off two-hour watches, and
when we could look across the valley and make out the
solid carved mass of the mountains against a scarcely
lighter sky we saddled up and started down, leading the
horses. Near the bottom we entered a pewter-colored
ground fog. The voices and the piano had stopped hours
before and we could actually hear the stuff sliding past our
pants legs like cats in the dark. We made as little stir as
six pairs of feet can. I had considered binding the horses'
hoofs with pieces of our jackets to hold down on noise, but
they made only little sucking sounds coming up out of the
half-congealed muck. The town smelled of beer and manure
and man-sweat and you could feel the silence coming back
at you off the dark walls of the buildings on either side.
There is no quiet like quiet in the mountains in the last
hour before light.

Dawn comes late there, but when it comes it comes all
in a bunch. The sun was an angry bloodshot eye in a pink
sky when we snaked behind a shoulder-high log smoke-
house and a crib smelling of chickens and came out behind
a rough corral with the blind wall of a board house closing
the fourth side. The door was an afterthought cut out of the
wall and hinged on the inside and you had to look hard to
see its thin outline, because it had neither outside handle
nor hole for a latchstring. It was a door made for going
out, not coming in. We were going to change all that.

The corral was gateless. You got the horses out by pulling the rails out of the rude holes in the posts to make an
opening. We tethered our mounts to the fence and climbed
over, setting our feet down carefully to avoid panicking the
half-dozen horses milling around inside. One of them was
a piebald, all right, and in the long shadows thrown by the

mountains to the east it looked like the Indian's. It snorted uneasily at the scent of me and moved to the other side of the corral, where its nervousness spread to the others. They stamped their forefeet and bobbed their heads and shook their manes and blew. I hoped we could get inside before someone came to see what was spooking them.

The back door opened then, and that was the end of the quiet in Teamstrike that day.

SIXTEEN

The open door threw a shadow over the figure on the threshold, but in its depths I made out a sheen of dull metal at hip height and the darker black of the hole bored down its length. I had my own gun out and the kid had his hand on his.

"I seen slower things," said Flynn, "but not lately."

Again we went through the ritual of putting up our weapons. It was getting redundant. Flynn stepped aside and we went in past him and he drew the door shut and shot the bolt. We were in a cramped, windowless room with a clay floor. Gray light leaked in around a poorly fitted inside door and touched a black iron cookstove and a woodbox and an ash can next to a broom and a mop. A long row of tired boots guarded one wall.

"Well?" I murmured. Whispers carried too far in sleeping households.

"Three rooms on the ground floor, not counting this and what Aunt Aurola calls the parlor," he replied in the same low tones. "I got a cot there. One's Aurola's and her hired girl's and two black prospectors share one and there's a fellow in the last looks a little like Sugar Jim, only skinnier, with a crooked jaw."

I said, "That'd be Harvey Byrd, Creel's cousin. The reader I saw in Helena said a horse kicked him once and broke it. What about the second floor?"

"Two rooms and a crawl space. Man in the north room's on the run from something. The Indian's got the one on the south end."

"You're sure it's the Indian?"

He nodded. "He come in two hours ago drunk with a woman hanging all over him. I was at the front door and I seen them heading for the stairs outside and it was too dark to see good, but he was talking too fast for his tongue like the Indian and it was the Indian's voice."

I breathed some damp morning air. Thinking. "Everyone tucked in?"

"I been here for the last hour and no one's come past me nor used the stairs since the Indian and his whore went up or I'd of heard it."

"You feeling up to taking Byrd?"

"Open-eyed or blindfolded?"

"Don't strut," I said. "He helped kill two good men. Give us to one hundred, then go tell Byrd it's time to get up."

"I'll be real gentle."

I drew back the bolt and told him to start counting as soon as we were out the door. The kid and I emerged slowly and moved along the back wall to keep distance between ourselves and the horses—one of which, now that the sun was higher, I recognized as Flynn's gray, still wearing its saddle and bridle with the reins thrown over the horn—and one by one we let ourselves over the fence. We crossed a sunken path leading to the outhouse behind the corral, rounded the side of the house and, guns drawn, started up the outside staircase slowly, leaning against the wall opposite the railing to avoid being seen from the single second-floor window and to keep the steps from complaining too loudly under our weight. Even so, the creaking seemed enough to bring half of Teamstrike down on us. We were on the east side of the house, climbing in direct sunlight across from a row of darkened buildings, and I felt like a cockroach on a white wall.

The staircase slanted from the front of the house to the back, with a balcony leading to two doors eight feet apart, the construction describing a large numeral seven on the wall. When we reached the balcony I signaled with my gun to the first door, behind which, according to Flynn, slept the stranger who was on the run from something. The kid nodded and stationed himself there holding his Colt. When things start happening it pays to have someone standing on those loose ends.

I flattened out against the wall between the doors and reached over to tap the Indian's with the barrel of the Deane-Adams.

The silence afterward stretched so long I was about to tap again when a voice called from inside.

"What do you want?"

It was the Indian, all right. I felt him clear down to my boots. I made my voice as harmless as his was thorny with suspicion. "Message." Well, it had worked on other occasions.

More silence. Then a rustling, as of weight coming off a corn shuck mattress, followed by the pad of bare feet on the other side of the door. Metal scraped metal and the door opened inward the width of a plain face with sagging cheeks and deep lines in the forehead, surrounded by wild tendrils of hair dyed bright red. The Indian's whore was wearing a man's faded flannel shirt clutched together at her neck and nothing else. I got my shoulder into the space while she was still looking and we went in together. She shrieked and I spun her around and got my left arm across her throat just as the Indian, standing stark naked next to the bed, curled a hand behind his head and flung the knife he kept in a sheath tied to a leather thong around his neck. The knife made a nasty noise in the air, ending in a nastier thump. The woman shuddered and then got too heavy to hold. I let her fall and squeezed off three rounds. The room throbbed and filled with smoke. Red blossoms opened on the Indian's chest, neck, and forehead. He went to his knees and then to his face and never said anything.

Just like that.

My ears hummed as if they'd been boxed. I looked down at the woman at my feet. She had slumped down and rolled half onto her back, the shirt opening to expose her poor naked body with all its sags and pouches and the obscene yellow-bone handle protruding between her breasts. While I was looking she breathed once, a long, shuddering intake. Then she stopped.

Someone was calling my name from a long way off. I shook myself and turned. The kid was standing where I'd left him, pointing his gun at a thickset man with sleep-tangled hair and gray chin stubble standing in the other doorway in stained red flannels with his hands in the air. Both of them were looking in the direction from which the shout had come.

"Murdock! Byrd's loose!"

It was Flynn calling. I saw a movement beyond the balcony, heard running footsteps, and saw the flapping open door of the outhouse, and then I knew where Harvey Byrd had been all the time we were thinking he was in his room waiting for Flynn to get the drop on him.

"I see him!"

The kid was pointing with his free hand, but the corner of the house blocked my view. I covered the man in the doorway and told the kid to shoot Byrd. He moved his gun that way and hesitated.

"Shoot!" I barked. "He's running for help."

The kid raised his gun and fired twice. I joined him on his end of the balcony in time to see a flash of white shirt vanish behind the corner of the building. Flynn's Colt opened up at the back, the shots sounding hurried. Then a space, and then a dog started barking. A door slammed somewhere and somewhere else someone shouted.

The man in red flannels grabbed for my gun. I backhanded the barrel across his face and he made a guttural noise and dribbled down the doorframe. I turned on the kid. "You hit anything at all?"

"I don't know. Maybe." He was trying to reload, but his hands were shaking so badly he kept missing the holes in the cylinder.

"What were you shooting at?"

"His legs."

"Christ, his legs."

More doors slammed. Dogs were barking all over the place now. I shoved the kid toward the stairs. The fresh cartridges squirted out of his hands and rattled to the balcony floor.

"Come on, come on. We're in rebel territory."

We scrambled down the stairs and around the corner, where Flynn was struggling to get a leg over his gray amid the other horses squealing and plunging in the corral. A hideously fat woman stood in the back doorway with matted gray hair to her shoulders and a man's worn robe not quite reaching around her bloated nakedness, her mouth scooping a black hole in her face, out of which a voice like a sustained blast on a steam whistle was calling for someone named Floss to hurry up with that goddamn shotgun.

"Couldn't get a clear shot at Byrd for the horses," Flynn

wheezed, uncoiling his reins from the horn. "He ran around the west side of the house."

"Hell with him." I slipped the sorrel's tether and lunged into the saddle. The kid was horsed already and leaned down to free his bay from the fence. There was a deep roar and suddenly his hat was snatched from his head as if by a gust of wind. Fat Aunt Aurola had her shotgun finally. She swung the second barrel on me and I aimed the Deane-Adams and shattered the doorframe next to her head. She howled and clapped a hand over her right eye, a splinter in it. Flynn took advantage of a clear space in the panicking horseflesh in the corral and raked his mount's ribs with his spurs and the gray screamed and bolted and sailed over the four-rail fence with an inch to spare. I gave him the lead and we galloped north. We were going to find out about his pass.

I glanced at the kid and saw blood streaking the side of his face. "Bad?" I asked.

"Caught a pellet or two in the forehead. The old lady's pattern had holes in it you could stick your hand through."

"Thought she had better sense'n to aim at something as thick as that," Flynn called back over his shoulder. His tone had a shallowness to it I didn't like.

The narrow cleft was granite on both sides, with pines growing halfway down the cliffs from clumps of grass and dirt on ledges where they had fallen from higher up and clung desperately. It was dark and chill there, as it would be every hour of the day except noon, when the sun shone briefly to the bottom. There were broad blasting scars in the walls, as Flynn had said; our horses skidded and stumbled on the loose rubble under their hoofs. We had to slow to a walk to avoid a spill. Not far behind us, quick hoof-beats bounded back and forth between the cliffs.

I steered with my knees and shook spent shells out of

my revolver, replacing them with cartridges from my belt. The kid kept looking back. "They'll have to slow down like us when they hit this part," I told him.

Flynn said, "If they stick as far as the Sag I'll pay you both a dollar. The Indian wouldn't of had a lot of that kind of friend."

"All he needed was one," I said. "Byrd."

"He won't be much for riding. He was favoring one leg running. It must of been him you hit when Creel and them jumped you and Miller and Rudabaugh."

Cocker Flynn's casual pose got to me sometimes. I said, "It didn't stop him from sneaking past you to the outhouse."

"He must of gone out the front and went around."

He paused for breath between words. "You all right?" I asked.

"Peachy," he said, and saying it, slid sideways out of his saddle.

I kicked the sorrel forward and caught him. My hand came away bloody from his side. I looked at the kid. "Ride."

He had drawn rein when Flynn started to fall. He looked at me dumbly. I had my gun in my free hand and I leveled the barrel across his horse's rump and pressed the trigger. The muzzle flame singed its coat. It reared and whinnied and pawed the air and took off bucking. The kid almost lost his seat as he rocked past. He sawed at the reins, but I sent another bullet whistling over the bay's head and it whinnied again and broke into a clean run, its shoes striking sparks off the treacherous loose rocks that paved the pass.

"You go too, Murdock."

The older lawman's voice was weak and muffled by my body. The effort of holding him up and keeping both horses under control put needles in my lower back.

"I like it here," I said.

"I ain't being no hero. I'm dead."

"We'll climb up to one of those ledges. We can hold them off from there until the kid gets back with help."

"I'm dead," he repeated.

And he was.

SEVENTEEN

I lowered him to the ground, hanging on to his collar, and when he was down I stepped out of leather and opened his coat. The side of his shirt and one pants leg were slick with blood. His stitches had to have been open for hours and he hadn't mentioned it. He had been too damn stubborn to admit his wounds would put him in the way. Cocker Flynn. Maybe not the first man to die of muleheadedness, but likely the best.

"First time you ever let me down, Flynn."

Scraping noises and curses down the pass put an end to the eulogy. In another few seconds they'd see me. I'd used up all my running and climbing time arguing with a dead man, and I had no cover. I looked at the sorrel and Flynn's gray. Well, that was why a wise man never named his horse. I shot mine behind the right ear and while it was still falling did the same for the other. The sorrel dropped fast, grunting. The gray threw up its broken head, knelt, and rolled over on top of its dead master with a shuddering sigh.

While the pass was still ringing with the reports I scrambled behind the new breastwork and got uncomfortable on my belly with my Winchester and Flynn's Spencer, rescued

from their saddle scabbards. I laid out two sacks of rifle
ammunition from the saddlebags and thumbed new cartridges into the Deane-Adams to replace the one I'd wasted
getting the kid's horse moving. Then I returned the revolver
to leather and cranked a shell into the Winchester's chamber and waited for bear.

Minutes marched past wearing heavy boots. In my
mind's eye I saw the men down the pass seek their own
cover from the sudden shots and then wait while the last
echo faded before moving forward afoot. Oblique sunlight
coming from the east capped the opposite side of the pass
in warm yellow, but the shadows at the bottom were still
as deep and clammy cold as a mine shaft and I wore out
my eyes looking for movement among the weird shapes of
moss-grown rocks and tree falls from above. Even then I
missed them when they came. One second I was looking
at a deserted stretch and the next it was crawling with men
in bulky jackets and hats with curled brims, holding out
their rifles for balance as they climbed over the rubble.

I steadied the Winchester's barrel across the dead sorrel's
rib cage and emptied the magazine, levering new rounds
up the pipe as fast as I fired. Lead spanged and squealed
off stone and sprayed granite dust and the men hurled themselves sideways and down and some of them returned fire
as they backed crouching into the shadows. A bullet
smacked the carcass I was hunkered behind.

I stopped shooting and dragged up the Spencer and
leaned it against the carcass while I reloaded the Winchester. Afterward I took advantage of the continued lull to lay
out my canteen and some strips of dried beef wrapped in
an oilskin I'd been carrying in one pocket. It was going to
be a long day.

                    •   •   •

Coming on noon the sun was high enough to bleach out the shadows. I saw a glint of metal among the boulders and upended roots slanting down from my position and then a buff-colored Stetson above that and drew a bead between the hat and the metal and fired and the hat went off at an angle, but beyond that I couldn't tell how good I'd made it because someone twelve feet to the right let go with a Springfield and I had to duck as the bullet screamed past my head. If you'd served with the army you never forgot that deep bellowing report. Throughout the noon hour I swapped shots with the Springfield and some lighter carbines farther down, the volleys short and brittle with pauses in between. Then the shadows crawled back in and things got quiet. I laid the Deane-Adams on top of the sorrel, which was starting to attract flies, and reloaded both rifles. I ate some meat and drank some water.

I was reaching for the revolver again when it went ping and leaped out of reach. The crack of the rifle was anticlimactic. The bullet had come from behind and to my right. I was stretched out on one hip and I hooked up the Spencer and twisted my torso that way.

"The buzzards'll pick your bones if you do."

The closeness of the voice arrested me. I looked up at the man crouched on a ledge thirty feet above with a Henry rifle against his right cheek. He was a lean specimen in a blue flannel shirt going gunmetal-colored in the sun and corduroy pants worn smooth at the knees and high black boots under a skin of dust. His flat-brimmed hat was tilted down to keep the sun out of his eyes and he had a ragged blond moustache tobacco-stained at the ends. I lowered the Spencer. He gestured with the barrel of the Henry and I lifted my hands.

"You get him, Blood?" called a harsh voice from down the pass.

"I got him. Come ahead."

Men rose from among the rocks and started forward with their carbines and rifles clapped to their hips, the muzzles leveled my way. I counted five out of the corner of my eye, but I was concentrating on the man with the Henry. A big black-bearded man wearing a gray Stetson and a denim jacket too short to cover a roll of red shirt spilling over his gun belt stooped with a grunt to pick up my revolver. He pointed it at me while a companion in an army coat bare of insignia stepped around the sorrel's carcass and collected the Spencer and Winchester. He had a repeating rifle of his own under one arm.

"Look to the other," said Black Beard.

Army Coat nudged Flynn's body with the muzzle of the Spencer. "Stiff as a stick."

"Come down, Blood."

Blood tossed the Henry to one of the others and climbed down from the ledge. Actually, it was a little later that I found out that was his name. The man with the black beard spoke with an accent and the way he pronounced it, it came out *Blut*. At the bottom the sharpshooter retrieved the repeater. The man he'd thrown it to carried a Springfield carbine. So far as I could see, no one in the group wore a belt gun, which wasn't unusual in that country.

"Who are you?" Black Beard asked me.

"Lillie Langtry."

The man in the army coat swung the butt of his own repeater and the left side of my head exploded. I came down on one shoulder and got a hand under me and started to rise. The rifle's single dead eye regarded me.

"Let him up," said Black Beard.

I got to my feet, swaying a little. My left ear rang.

"Search him."

Army Coat leaned all three long guns against the base

of the cliff and knocked up my elbows and patted me down.
His face was young and clean-shaven and might have been
nice to look at before a horse or something just as heavy
had stepped on his nose. He found the deputy's star Flynn
had given me in my breast pocket and showed it to Black
Beard.

"Well," said the latter, not unpleased. "It appears we
have us some law here. You killed a good man today, Mr.
Law. Clarence down there ate that bullet you sent him but
it didn't agree with him."

"Two men," one of the others corrected sullenly. "You
forgot the Indian."

I glanced at the speaker. Middle height, fair, long burn-
sides, jaw slightly out of skew. But for that, Harvey Byrd
was a close match with his cousin in the Helena jail. He
had on a hat with a tall crown and the brim curling in on
itself and a white shirt and striped pants and stood cradling
a battered Winchester with most of his weight on his right
leg.

"I said a *good* man. But Teamstrike takes care of its
own." Black Beard was still looking at me. "I asked you
before what your name was. You don't have to give it to
me if you think it's worth dying for where you stand."

I gave it to him. Something came into his neutral-colored
eyes, but aside from that he made no sign of recognition.
"Let's get this done," he said to the others.

"Town?" asked Army Coat.

"The Sag, where someone will find him. Folks have to
know who owns Montana."

Byrd said, "What about the other one? There was three
in town."

"Forget him. Where will he go? We have that toy sheriff
in Great Falls buffaloed and he'll not find help between
there and Helena. If that bastard judge is fool enough to

send more men we'll do them too. Then maybe he'll know to stick to his town like we had to to ours for so long."

He spat the words *bastit jutch* into my face. He was as German as they come.

"Looky here." Byrd, who had been going through the dead sorrel's saddlebags, held up my manacles. The key was in the lock.

"See if they fit Murdock," Black Beard said.

"Front or back?"

"Front. He has to ride."

Byrd laid down his Winchester and wrenched my arms into position and made the cuffs bite. He put the key in his breast pocket with exaggerated care and cracked me across the face with the back of his hand. I staggered back a step and kicked him in the groin.

He bent double, coughing and retching. His face was the shade of cave mold. Army Coat and the man called Blood stepped in and grabbed my arms.

"Hold on to him," croaked Byrd. His color was return-ing in fever patches. He scooped up his carbine and swung it by the barrel.

Black Beard hit him hard with his thick shoulder, tearing loose what wind remained in Byrd's lungs with a loud *woof*. Byrd stumbled backward over Cocker Flynn's body and went down. The Winchester clattered on the rocks.

"It's better when they're alive," Black Beard told him. He was breathing heavily from the effort of moving so much bulk so fast.

The man with the Springfield had gone down the pass and now he came back up leading seven horses. He was my age, tall and bony, and wore gold-rimmed spectacles with strips of cloth tied around the earpieces to keep them from digging into flesh. The two men holding me shoved me up to a middle-sized dun that presumably had belonged to dead Clarence. I stirruped and grasped the saddle horn in my manacled hands and got aboard.

The last man in the party had almond-shaped eyes tilted like a Mongol's and half-inch triangles of black moustache at the corners of his mouth. He kicked one of Flynn's stiff legs. "What about Clarence and this one?"

"You and Shiloh drag them out of the way and get some rocks on top of them," said Black Beard, straddling a big black that grunted when he let his weight down on it. "Get a rope on the horses and do the same. We don't want buzzards marking the spot. Catch up with us when you're finished. Harvey and Specs will ride with me. You too, Blood. Mount up."

"Second." Blood who had evidently removed his spurs in order to make his way around behind me quietly, was buckling them back on over his insteps. They were the Mexican kind, with long, cruel rowels.

EIGHTEEN

Schichter was the name of the big German with the black beard. He and Blood and Clarence the dead man and the one they called Shiloh—that had to have something to do with his army coat, which was the only thing about him old enough to have seen that battle—had stuck up an Over-land stagecoach in southern Wyoming for five thousand in gold last December, killing the driver and fleeing north. They had lost the gold when their packhorse slipped during the Missouri crossing, but had hopes of recovering the strongbox when the waters went down. Meanwhile they had holed up in Teamstrike. Blood had gotten drunk there and spilled the gold story to Specs and the Mongol-eyed one they called Chink, both of whom were wanted elsewhere, and now they were partners.

A sheriff from the Bear's Paw Mountain country had become the stranglers' first victim when he collared Specs outside Teamstrike and took him back to stand trial for the rape and murder of a Shoshone woman in his jurisdiction. Chink alerted Schichter and the others, reminding them of the lost gold that bound them, and they rode down and hanged the sheriff ten miles short of his destination. After that, Specs and Chink had reciprocated by helping Schi-

chter's band string up two Pinkerton agents who had
tracked the stage robbers from Wyoming.

Harvey Byrd and the Indian had come late to the party.
After they ambushed my posse, the Indian had seen to
Byrd's wounded leg and run to cover with him in the out-
law town, where the Indian happened to match the print of
a cracked horseshoe he had conveniently forgotten to mention to me at the site of the Pinkerton lynching to its original in a corral. When he found out the horse belonged to
Shiloh he had approached him with his knowledge. At that
point the gang swelled to eight, more than enough to jump
Cocker Flynn and the Swede and the two deputies from
Great Falls when they came looking for the Indian and
Byrd. They were all killers and they trusted one another as
much as sharks in a feeding frenzy, which was why none
of them had managed to dispose of any of the others. "Yet,
anyway," added Blood, who told me the whole story on
the way through the pass to the Shonkin Sag. A man who
likes to talk will tell you anything when he knows you
won't be repeating it.

"You forgot one," I said. "There was a railroad detective hanged near Fort Benton month before last."

"Wasn't ours." He grinned. "Reckon we ain't the only
stranglers working this part of the woods."

Schichter, riding alone up front, called back for Blood to
shut it.

We were not quite abreast, Blood hanging back some
astride a chestnut mare with his Spanish-style hat still tilted
down over his eyes and the Henry across the throat of his
saddle. Byrd and Specs rode shoulder to shoulder between
us and the German. Whenever that bunch went anywhere,
it must have been hell's own hassle deciding who would
be at whose back. We had left the rockfalls behind and
were coming up from between the cliffs along a hogback

with the land falling off sharply on either side and the razor
tops of sixty-foot pines stabbing up at us from below. We
could see the Missouri, not brown at this distance but steel-
blue, snaking through the tablelands with dense forest all
around and sky a hundred miles high and to the west a
wiggly blue line that was the Rockies with the sun swelling
and flushing hot orange just over the summit. There were
no clouds to reflect the sunset, just a coppery strip along
the horizon behind the mountains. I looked at it, remembered it. You never know when you will see another.

Schichter was mad. You hear all the time about men
going crazy but it's just a word until you see it. He had
started out with greed for gold and a keen instinct for sur-
vival and ended up seeing himself as some kind of frontier
warlord. He was convinced his random murders had the
law quaking and was determined to make the Montana bad-
lands his fiefdom. So much open space could warp a man
too long from civilization; most times it shrank him with
the heart-sickening realization of his own insignificance,
but sometimes it worked opposite, the room to grow in any
direction and the sensation of breathing air no one had
breathed before charging his brain like a strong drug. I
doubted that Schichter still thought about the stolen gold.
Blood did, and probably so did Specs and Chink and Shiloh, though I couldn't say about Harvey Byrd. That they
stuck with the German said something for the mental hold
he had on them. It was a thing that went with madness like
dark with a doused lamp.

The long hump of land descended gradually into a saddle
and then the true sink of the Sag, thorny with pine and
cedar, with puddles like pieces of bright metal reflecting
sky at the bottom from the spring runoff. Although the sun
was still visible above the Rockies, it was already growing
dark at the base of the ancient channel. Peepers stopped

singing and plopped into the water at our approach.

I knew which tree it was going to be as soon as I saw it. A lone maple stood in a patch of ground cleared by a trapper whose grandchildren were grandparents by now, his cabin rotting kindling sunken into its stone foundation with seedlings six feet high all around. The tree's trunk was just broad enough to hug and its lowest limb made an elbow twelve feet above the ground to avoid the older, larger trees on the edge of the clearing. Schichter drew rein and held up a hand. Byrd and Specs stopped and Blood spurred past me and reached over and took my dun by the bit chain, halting it. Shiloh and Chink had caught up with us by then. They walked their horses around us and slacked off the reins and let them graze. On every side birds were singing.

No one spoke. Specs, his glasses white in a stray sunbeam, unhooked a coil of rope from his saddle horn and fashioned a noose on the end for weight and with the coil in one hand and the noose end in the other, made a series of expert twirls, feeding out rope between his thumb and his palm, and swung the noose up over the limb. It didn't have enough behind it on the first try and fell back, skidding off the bark. He reeled it in and made some more revolutions and threw it again and this time the noose described a clear high arc and came down on the other side trailing six feet of rope. He tossed the rest of the coil to Shiloh, who caught it and kneed his horse forward and bent down to pass it around the tree and pull two feet off the dangling part and secure the other end, leaning back with a grunt to set the knot. Specs meanwhile had made a better job of the noose, although there was nothing of the thirteen tight coils that snapped a man's neck clean at a proper hanging. Clean deaths held no interest for this crew.

Black-bearded Schichter, looking like a bear in a man's clothes, watched the operation from horseback with a fore-

man's critical eye. He looked at Blood, who was still holding my horse's bit, and Blood put heels to his and we
moved ahead. I was between him and Harvey Byrd now,
the latter sitting a dun that was a little larger than mine.
Specs waited holding the noose.

My right boot was out of its stirrup. I kicked Blood very
hard in the armpit where he was leaning over to guide my
mount and he made an awful reverse croak of a noise and
I raked the dun's ribs and shot forward, sideswiping Byrd
and charging through the space between Specs and Schichter. I was shouting something without words in it at the
top of my lungs. I hoped it was as paralyzing as an Indian's
war cry. Someone shouted something equally unintelligible
behind me—it sounded like German—and a shot was fired,
but go hit a moving target with a rifle from horseback. I
was making for the west bank that led up and out of the
Sag. Pine branches larruped my face and snatched off my
hat. Swift cold air stung the lacerations on my cheeks and
roared past my ears.

Hoofs pounded earth behind me. I had the reins in both
manacled hands and snapped them, digging my heels into
horseflesh and hunkering down for speed. The dun was
throwing lather that burned like alcohol when it flew into
my eyes. The pursuing hoofbeats got louder.

A cannonball struck me from behind and to the left, rip-
ping me out of the saddle, and together the cannonball and
I fell and fell with trees and sky blurring past, and then we
stopped with a shattering blow that numbed my right side
and tore my lungs inside out.

Byrd recovered first. I had broken his fall after he'd
launched himself into me from horseback, and now he got
his hands around my throat and squeezed, his crooked face
a violent mask two inches from mine in the failing light

with his eyes starting and his lips skinned back from the offset rows of his teeth.

"Murdering bastard," he was saying in a high, keening whine. "Murder Melrose and take Jim and murder the Indian."

I wrenched onto my left shoulder hard, unseating him, got an elbow in his ribs and pushed and felt something start to give and his grip loosened on my neck a notch and I butted him in the face with my head and we came apart then. He got to his feet first because my bound hands got in the way of my balance, and threw a kick at my head, but it was his bad leg and he couldn't put his weight behind it. His boot grazed my forehead and I reached up and grabbed his leg and pulled and he was down again. This time we rose together. He swung his fist. I ducked it and butted him again, in the chest this time, and when he bent wheezing I swung my laced hands in an uppercut and caught him square on the point of the chin. Something crunched and he straightened out and tipped over backward and lay on the ground moaning through a jaw broken the second time. Then he put a hand on the ground and started to get back up.

There was a sharp crack and a blue-black hole spoiled his forehead and his head snapped back and he toppled off his knees and didn't try to get up again.

I pivoted. Blood was standing on the edge of the trapper's clearing with the Henry to his cheek and smoke twisting out the end of the barrel. While I was looking he swung it a few inches to the right to cover me. Chink and Shiloh rode through the studding of pines and wheeled behind me and pushed me ahead of them using their horses' shoulders. My dun and Byrd's were still running.

"Harvey was no fun to have around without the Indian

to stop his yelping,'' said Schichter, still sitting his black where I had left him. "Chink, his hands."

Chink rode back to Byrd's body and got the key and rode in. He dismounted, sprang the cuffs, and locked them again when he had my hands behind my back. He wasn't any rougher about it than he had to be. His kind didn't hate. When you had your chance you killed them first. When he was finished he let the key drop to the needle-matted ground.

Blood had lowered the Henry. Now he thumped the muzzle hard into my chest. I had to backpedal to keep from stumbling and bumped into his mare behind me. The horse snorted and sidestepped. "Get up there," he said.

The way his left arm hung suggested it was dislocated at the shoulder.

"I don't think so," I said.

He came forward and thumped my chest again. His mare shook its mane and put more distance between us.

I said, "If you want to lynch me you can damn well sweat a little and haul me up from the ground. Nothing says I have to make it easy."

Schichter said, "If you refuse to mount I will have Specs drop the noose over your head where you stand and drag you. I don't know if that's worse or better than hanging, but it takes longer."

"*I'll* drag him," Blood volunteered.

It was getting hard to see. Shiloh produced a lantern and struck a match. An early moth flung itself against the glass as soon as it started to glow. I wondered if it was the same lantern Cocker Flynn had seen that first night. It was a shame the stranglers hadn't recognized him by day as the man they had shot and left for dead. They'd have thought he was some kind of spook. Blood held his horse and I got a boot into the stirrup. Chink gave me a boost up because

I couldn't grip the horn with my hands behind me.

The air was cooling rapidly, the way it will up there at night until well into the summer. The sweat I had worked up wrestling with Harvey Byrd was icy under my clothes. The saddle under me was cold and slippery stiff and the chestnut mare was shivering a little under the chilling froth of its half-day journey. All the birds were through singing. It was just me and the stranglers and the horses and crawly yellow light from the lantern and the *chee-chee-chee* of ground frogs that whenever a man heard it for the rest of his life would take him back to that night.

"It takes three minutes to choke to death," Schichter was saying in his flat foreman's voice. "I guess it must seem longer to the one doing the choking. None of us thought to tie that sheriff's hands behind him up in the Bear's Paw and when we walked his horse out from under him he reached up and hung on until his arms went dead and his fingers just kind of slipped off the rope. You ought to be glad we've learned from our mistakes."

While the German was talking, Specs leaned over from his saddle and hooked the noose over my head and snugged what knot there was up under my left ear. I had lost my hat in the fight with Byrd. The rope felt stiff and rough as burrs around my throat. Blood was still holding the horse.

"If you have something to say we will hear it," Schichter said.

"Go to hell."

"I hope you will save me a place in line." He nodded to Blood, who led the mare forward.

I kept my seat as long as I could, my thigh muscles tighter than they'd ever been, but the saddle slid smoothly between them and the stirrups hung up on my cramped toes only long enough for Chink on the ground and Specs on horseback to pull them loose. My heels grazed the chestnut's rump. And then there was just air under me and black sky above with stars punched in it.

NINETEEN

It was an eerie weightless feeling, suspended in vaulted night with cold air coming up under my pants legs and the part of my brain that understood gravity shrieking that this was all wrong. The rope was iron on my neck and I felt my tongue sliding out and my eyes straining at their sockets and my vision shrank to pinpoints with purple all around, the faces of Specs and Schichter and Shiloh on horseback in the lantern glow sharply detailed, as if seen through a strong lens. Then the pinpoints closed and I was in total darkness. I heard loud popping noises and knew they were made by blood vessels exploding in my head. Then I heard nothing, felt nothing. Instead I dreamed.

Dreamed that I was trapped inches below the surface of a swift river, caught in the undertow and hurtling along, bumping into horses and things standing stationary in the current and sliding around them and tumbling down a cataract, unable to grab on to anything along the way because my hands were manacled behind me. The cold water was numbing and I barely felt the impacts as I bounded off rocks and limbs and horses' legs and went on with my lungs bursting and fishes and flotsam skidding past my face. The empty hollow of my skull echoed.

"Murdock. Come on, Murdock. Come on."

I was in a slower part of the river, less cold, with more things floating in it and patting my face and sunlight refracting down through the water and splintering into colors as if through a prism. There were horses standing here too, their legs all around me. *Come on, Murdock* kept echoing and the floating things were alive and slapping my face and making my cheeks burn. I opened my eyes and the kid's narrow anxious face with its pillow-fuzz of neglected beard was looking down at me through the shifting water. I warned him about the undertow but my mouth filled with water and nothing came out. He slapped me again.

"You're all right, Murdock," he said. "We cut you down and you're all right."

I moved my eyes and they made grating sounds in their sockets and ached. There were horses' legs all around me and other faces a mile up under hats whose wide brims trapped the lantern light. One of the faces belonged to someone I had met a long time ago. The sheriff from Great Falls?

I was lying on my back on a patch of moist cold earth. Beyond the high faces the bent white arm of the tree I had swung from reached up to cup the sky in naked fingers with a rag of old hemp dangling from its elbow.

White muslin diagonaled the kid's forehead where someone might have popped Aunt Aurola's shotgun pellets loose with a knife. I dragged a dry tongue over lips like old leaves, but my throat closed up on the first word.

"Talk later," he said. "We thought you had a crushed pipe, but you're breathing all right now. You weren't at all when we cut you down. Your face was as black as my boot."

"First thing you should do when you get so you can talk is thank the kid," said the sheriff. He was wearing a patched buffalo jacket on top of his coveralls and had traded his short scattergun for a Spencer carbine. He had a cold and his nose was running into his coal-smear of beard. "He got the drop on me out where I was digging and talked me into rounding up a posse and heading for Teamstrike. He didn't want tending, but them greasy pellets infect quick and halfway here we held him down and done the job. We hit the Sag about the time they fired that lantern. By the time we got dismounted and close enough to use our rifles, these here was too busy watching you twist to mind us. We got every damn one of 'em."

I cranked myself up on one elbow and looked around. I had a stiff neck to go with my sore throat and aching head. "These here" were Schichter and Shiloh and Specs and Blood, shadowy bales lying where they had fallen in the dirty glow from the lantern burning low on the ground, recognizable mostly by their clothes, although you couldn't miss the German's supine bulk. Specs' glasses lay on the ground near his body, one smashed lens twinkling. The front of Shiloh's army coat smoldered and gave off a foul stench of burning wool and cooking meat. The sheriff saw me notice it.

"He wanted to make a fight of it with a bullet in one arm and two in his back already. I obliged him at six feet."

Someone was missing. I did some more looking around and the sheriff read my thoughts again.

"That one slunk off gutshot into the woods. The kid went in after him and come back alone."

I looked at the kid, but he was busy unstopping a canteen and you had to have been studying his hands and seen the slight tremor. I would not have followed someone like Chink into the woods; but there would be time to talk about that later. I took the canteen from the kid while he was trying to tip it up to my lips and did it myself. The cold

water washed a channel down my burning throat. My neck
was swollen and felt as if the noose were still drawn tight
around it and when I was finished drinking I put a hand
there to make sure. My fingertips found the braided imprint
in the flesh. The burn scar would be with me for a while,
and maybe forever. My hands felt hot too and I realized
that it was from returning circulation and that I wasn't
wearing manacles anymore.

"We had the devil's own time finding where they
dropped the key," explained the kid.

I took another drink and said, "They're the ones that
lynched your friend Chubb Bowles and your other deputy,
Sheriff." It came out a croaked whisper.

"Figured as much." There was nothing in the peace of-
ficer's tone.

The kid said, "Flynn?"

I shook my head. He nodded. "Bury them?" he asked
the sheriff.

"I reckon we got to, or be no better than them."

There were eight in the posse besides the sheriff and the
kid, all deputized prospectors. Two of them produced shov-
els and they leaned into them with ease and in almost less
time than it takes to tell about it they had a common grave
dug six feet down and eight feet wide and dumped them in
without ceremony. Someone fetched Byrd's corpse and the
kid went into the woods carrying the lantern and hauled
back Chink's body with his coat and shirt bunched up
around his chest and his dead Mongol eyes contemplating
the sky. He went in on top of the pile and soon it was
covered with dirt and the kid got out his pocket Bible and
read something short from the Old Testament. I was up now
and testing my legs. Remarkable things, legs. Also arms
and hands and fingers. You get to thinking such things
when your life's been pulled away and then put back. I

found the noose end of the rope lying where someone had
flung it after I was cut down and I used my pocket knife
to saw off a three-inch piece and stuck it in a pocket.

"Souvenir?" asked the kid, joining me.

"Reminder."

The sheriff told his men to collect the rifles and carbines
and those horses that hadn't run off during the shooting.
"What we get for them and the gear should take care of
posse pay," he added to the kid and me. I didn't care.
Cutting me down entitled them to everything in the Highwoods.

We camped on some high ground west of the Sag, with
a bottle of whiskey going around a big fire along with
tinned sardines and squares of salt pork. I passed on the
food and let the raw whiskey cauterize my throat. Already
they were talking about bullets nicking twigs and things
just over their heads. Years later they would haul out tired
old coats and hats growing mildew and poke their fingers
through moth holes by way of showing how close they
came to the edge that night, and they wouldn't be lying,
because by then they'd believe every word. Someone lent
me a blanket and we slept until first light and then drank
hot coffee and mounted up for the trip back to Great Falls.
I rode the chestnut mare I had so much not wanted to leave
before. In town the kid and I picked up some stores and
shook hands with the sheriff and were out of there by early
afternoon. We overnighted at Painted Rock, where the kid's
father heard our story at the supper table with his moustache grim and said nothing except to demand coffee from
his young wife. My throat had opened up by then and I
was eating.

In the morning the kid came out to the barn where I was
saddling the chestnut and said, "I won't be going on to
Helena with you. I'll send someone in a day or so to pay

me up at the hotel and collect my things and what you think
you owe me.''

"Oh?" I leaned the cinch tight.

"Pa needs me here. Every time I go away and come back
he looks older. He's got rheumatism and his eyes are going,
though he won't own up to it. The ranch will fly all to hell
if I don't start looking after things.''

"That's dust." I scabbarded my Winchester. Shiloh had
taken good care of it. I didn't know what had become of
Flynn's Spencer. The sheriff had taken my Deane-Adams
off Schichter's body and returned it, too.

"Yeah," the kid admitted. "It's dust. Maybe I ain't cut
out for ranching, but I was a damn fool to try marshaling
a second time.''

I looked at him across the saddle. He went on.

"That gutshot one went sliding in through them trees
and didn't make a noise, just like a wounded cougar. I went
in after him in the dark. I stopped with black trees and
bushes all around and it was just as quiet—well, the peepers had stopped and after all that shooting it was like it is
just after a bell stops ringing. I was holding my Colt. I
heard a rustling and I swung that way and snapped off a
shot and a buck deer blatted and thumped the ground going
away, crashing through the bushes. I reckon that's why I
was a little slower turning the next time I heard something.

"He come straight at me then, all movement in the dark
with his breath whistling and I had the Colt pointed right
at him and I didn't even remember I had it, I couldn't
move. He ran into me and I went over backwards. He
grabbed my gun by the barrel and I was falling down away
from him and he was pulling the gun back toward him and
it went off and he kind of shuddered then, and by that time
I had one foot behind the other and I pulled the hammer
back with both thumbs and shot him again and then his

fingers just kind of slid off my hands on the gun. He grunted when he hit the ground, just like a grizzly blowing its lungs when you stop its charge.''

I was still looking at him, but I couldn't read his expression in the barn doorway with the sun at his back.

"It got even quieter then," he said. "There wasn't any wind at all and I was choking on spent powder. I tried to get a light going. I went through almost every match I had before I got one struck, and there he was on the ground in front of me, laying on his stomach with his head turned on one side. I squatted with the Colt in one hand and the match in the other and looked at his face. His mouth was clamped tight with blood in one corner and his eyes was going soft. They kept getting softer the longer I looked at them. Just like any dead animal's.''

"The first five are the hardest," I said, and was conscious of having said it before when I was a lot younger.

"I reckon I'll take your word on that.''

I led the horse out into the sunshine and mounted. The kid had come with me and I leaned down to grasp his hand.

"You were a help twice," I said. "You know where I am if you ever need some back.''

He smiled with the sun on his face. "Don't wait for it. I mean to live quiet and die of boredom.''

"For whatever price you put on it I think you decided right.''

"You feel that way, what keeps you doing it?''

"I'm pretty good at it," I said. "When I'm not blundering into ambushes and getting my neck stretched and my friends killed.''

"I reckon you liked Flynn.''

"He was a damn fool and came as close to killing us all as you can come and still not do it. Yes, I liked him.'' I

held up a hand and he held one up and I snicked the mare
forward with the sun at my back.

I welcomed the warmth of it on my way around the Big
Belts. The air was sweet now with spring to stay and one
of those chinooks that brush your face like a woman's fingers was coming in over the Rockies all the way from Ne-
vada. My neck and throat were better but I still had the
headache. It felt as it might have had those popping noises
I'd heard while I was hanging really been the sound of my
blood vessels bursting and not gunfire from the Great Falls
posse. Also my wrists were sore from all those hours wearing manacles.

The light was almost gone when I crossed the Missouri
and swung left, bypassing Helena entirely for Judge Blackthorne's house a mile outside of town. When you've left a
place in unfamiliar hands it's only common sense to find
out what those hands have been up to before you go back.
A lamp was burning downstairs when I groundhitched the
mare and stepped up on the porch.

"Murdock!"

I turned around slowly, quietly drawing the Deane-
Adams as I did so, with my body between it and the man
who had hailed me. The lawn in front of the house was
dark and the man standing there was wearing a tan Texas
hat whose wide brim threw his face in shadow from the
light coming through the window from inside, but I recognized his black clothes and the Colt in his hand and most
of all his whispery wheeze of a voice. His new deputy's
star gleamed sullenly on his breast.

TWENTY

"Hello, Willard," I said. "Where's the Colonel?"

"Don't know. Don't care. These days I answer to Marshal Mercy."

"What's your business here?"

"Protecting the judge."

"From what?"

"Visitors. Marshal's orders."

The gun was a rock in his hand. I held the Deane-Adams close to my hip out of sight. "That include me?"

"You especially," he said. "I'm arresting you."

"What's the charge?"

"That's up to the marshal. Come down off of there slow."

"It's dark. You'll have to show me the way."

Silence stretched thin and tight between us. Then the light found something on his face . . . A smile?

"Your choice." He twirled and holstered the six-gun and set his feet with his arms bent and I shot him twice in the thickest part of his body.

The first bullet staggered him. The second knocked him sitting, as .45s will no matter where you hit them. He sat on the grass with his fingers laced on his chest and the blood dark between them and his hat was off now and the light on his face was yellow. "That wasn't fair," he gasped.

"Who said anything about fair?"

The front door opened while I was watching him die. I spun, thumbing back the hammer. Judge Blackthorne was standing just inside in his shirtsleeves, collarless, with the light behind him.

"I thought that was your English gun," he said. "It has a nasty sound. Is he dead?"

I started to say not yet, but by the time I turned back and looked at Frank Willard again the answer had changed. He had flopped over onto his right shoulder with his hands still on his chest and his gun still in its holster. Blackthorne stepped out on the porch, drawing the door shut behind him. "Was that necessary?"

"It would have been later if not now," I said. "He was too fast."

The Judge looked grim. "He and Jericho Mercy have been holding us here for three days, spelling each other. They took my Remington first thing."

"How's Mrs. Blackthorne?"

"She's upstairs. She took a sleeping potion. What happened with the Indian?"

That was the Judge for you, business first no matter what. I told him the whole thing there on that ghostlit porch with a dead man lying just off the edge. Blackthorne scowled in his neat beard.

"Why is it Sugar Jim Creel is the only man you've brought in alive in months?"

"My neck feels all right now," I said. "Thanks for asking."

He ignored that. "Creel hangs next month for the surveyor's murder. The jury came in divided on the murders of Miller and Rudabaugh.''

"I don't guess that matters with the Indian and Byrd dead.''

"Not to you.''

I ignored *that*. "What's Mercy up to?''

"What you said. He's stuck a straw into everything in Helena that tastes like money and levied a two-percent tax on all the gold that comes through the assay office. He started by sending every available deputy but his brothers and Willard west on some trumped-up posse and then he placed Bill Gordon and me under house arrest, calling it protection. If you hadn't come here first he or Joshua or Jericho or all three would probably have cut you down as soon as your first shoe hit the street.''

"Didn't anybody stand up to them?''

"Just two, Chicago Joe and the owner of the Belmont. Mercy padlocked the Belmont for improper disposal of slops, but now it's open again and you figure it out. One of Joe's girls got knocked around by a customer, though she won't say who it was, and now Joe is paying too.''

"Which girl?''

"A young blonde. I think they call her Jackie. She's pretty badly broken up.'' He peered at my face. "What's wrong?''

"It's the light here,'' I said. "Does Mercy still hang out at the Belmont?''

"Yes, but—''

"Mr. Murdock.''

The harsh whisper came from beyond the light shed through the window. I had put away my gun and now I drew it again and moved so that I wasn't outlined against the lighted square of glass. "Who's talking?''

A pause, and then something small glittered out of the

darkness and tinkled onto the boards at my feet. I nudged
it with a toe. It was my deputy's star, the one I had given
to Duncan, the Negro who ran the livery.

"Come ahead," I said. "If you're alone."

"I been alone since I was borned." He stepped into the
light, a thick hard man with dull gray hair in tight coils,
wearing the same filthy shirt and jeans I had seen him in
last. When I saw he was alone I put up the revolver and
squatted and picked up the star and stood and put it in my
breast pocket.

"I been watching the place the last two nights," Duncan
said. "I figured if you came at all you'd come here and
after dark." He kicked Frank Willard's body at his feet.
"You don't look so much now, Mr. Scourge of the Border."

"It costs nothing to respect the dead," said the Judge
sternly.

"Yes, sir."

"What is it?" I asked the Negro.

"The Mercys is waiting for you in town. They been expecting you the last couple of nights like me. Jericho, he's
by your room. Joshua's at the livery and Jordan's in the
Belmont like always." He showed the spaces between his
teeth. "Attila's got Rome and you're outside the wall."

"I knew that, or suspected it. What else?"

"I'm thinking you're wanting to get in there without
making a lot of noise about it. I'm thinking I can help."

"I'm listening."

"Don't be an idiot," said the Judge. "Before they
trapped me here I wired Cheyenne for marshals. Let them
handle it."

I said, "If Mercy's got things nailed down as tight as
you say he knows all about that wire. Those marshals will
be the best part of a month getting their orders straight and

outfitting and riding here. By that time he and his brothers will have made their strike and gone. Talk," I told Duncan.

"Best way to cover noise is make a louder one," he said. "I got me a fair noisemaker right here."

He reached behind his back and pulled something out from under his belt and brought it around in front. It was a pre–Civil War pepperbox pistol, .36 caliber, brass and steel with a walnut grip, six-barreled and big as a general store.

He said, "I gots to be careful with it, on account of the flash sets off the other five caps sometimes and she sprays lead like a Gatling."

"What do you gain by this?" I asked him.

"I'm fifty-two and black, Mr. Murdock. I don't stand to lose a whole hell of a lot, if you'll excuse my bad language, Judge, your honor."

That didn't answer my question, but I told him to give me the rest of it. He shrugged.

"I'm thinking if somebody was to ride through town apopping away with Old Sally here, somebody else could slip in while everybody was looking the wrong way."

"No good. The Mercys are smarter than they are honest. They won't leave their posts just for that."

While I was talking, Duncan stepped over Willard's body and mounted the porch. "They might if they thought it was you doing the riding and popping," he said, and transferred my hat from my head to his. He grinned his checkered grin.

Blackthorne said, "You're idiots, the two of you," and went inside, closing the door gently to avoid waking his wife.

Duncan had walked from town. We led the mare in silence the mile to the town limits, where I slipped out of my canvas jacket and he put it on to go with my hat and I handed him the reins. "Can you count to a thousand?" I asked.

"When I got to. Generally I don't see a thousand of much of anything."

"Count to that and then ride like hell. Don't start firing that widow-maker until you're at least halfway to the end of the street. Then get rid of it because the iron will just slow you down, and squeeze everything you can out of the chestnut. Find some place to overnight and don't come back before morning."

I stopped talking. We were standing at the mouth of the broad main street with light scalloping the edges from the windows of brick buildings on both sides. Piano music trickled out of the saloons, but at the moment the street was deserted. With all the regular deputies out of town there were no figures in the shadows with shotguns. I clasped Duncan's hand, crusty with calluses.

"Stay alive," I said.

"You too."

I left him to wind my way down alleys reeking of slops and behind frame buildings with the paint eaten down to the wood where stray dogs had lifted their legs against them. Everything looks different at night and I made a wrong turn that sent me a block off course, but I doubled back and came out behind the livery. An orange glow the size of a nickel marked where Joshua Mercy was smoking a cigar at the other end of the alley. While I was looking, the glow made an upward arc and brightened, reflecting off the highlights of his broad fleshy face with its thick dark moustache curling at the ends. Threads of smoke uncoiled under a coal-oil streetlamp on the corner.

Keeping to the shadows I moved along the back wall of the gunsmith's shop that faced the street perpendicular to the one the livery was on, leaning on the balls of my feet and feeling in front of me with each foot to make sure there were no obstacles in my path. It took me well past the count of a thousand to get around the long building, but Duncan must have been a slow counter, because just as I reached the corner around from Joshua, close enough to smell his cigar, hoofs thudded in the direction of Main Street and then a harsh flat snapping shattered the relative silence, the noise of a .36 pistol being fired in the open air.

"What the hell!" I heard Joshua say, and then he came past the corner with his profile against the light from the streetlamp and one hand reaching back for the Smith & Wesson in his holster. I had the Deane-Adams by the barrel in my right hand and I brought the butt down square into the center of his black hat as hard as I had ever hit anything. He whimpered a little and dropped like a sack full of anvils.

TWENTY-ONE

I reached down to jerk his gun out of leather, but he had fallen on top of it and I couldn't find the butt under his two hundred and forty-plus pounds. Doors were slamming and dogs were barking and people were shouting. It was Teamstrike all over again. A six-gun coughed deeply Main Street way. I heard footsteps approaching on the run and turned and grasped the handle of one of the big front doors to the stable and pulled it and it was unlocked and I ducked through the opening and let the door close behind me, muffling the noises outside.

The darkness inside made the air seem cooler. The place stank of ammonia and liniment and mildewed straw and when I closed my eyes there was no difference in light. But light must have been leaking in from somewhere, because after a few seconds I could make out the solid blackness of the stalls against the general dark and the aisle of earth running between them. The horses sensed me and moved restlessly in their stalls. I felt my way through to the back with my gun in my hand and turned and faced the big doors.

Going back over it later, I calculated my wait to be only a few minutes, but in the crushing gloom of that stable it seemed as if dawn would break soon when I heard voices outside.

"Josh! Are you all right, Josh?"

"He all right?"

"His head is bleeding. Josh?"

Slapping noises. A groan.

"He's c-coming around."

More slapping. "What happened, Josh? Who hit you?"

A pause, then: "He didn't get around to introducing himself." Joshua's voice sounded like a phonograph cylinder winding down.

There was a general scuffling and heavy breathing and one of the doors creaked as if something heavy was leaning against it.

"Are you well?"

I recognized Jordan Mercy's careful English. Joshua said something back in his wound-down tone that I didn't catch.

"Let's g-get the horses." This was Jericho.

Someone shushed him. There was a long stretch broken into whispered sibilants. Then nothing, and then a rusty hinge gasped and a vague grayish rectangle ten feet high and two feet wide opened in the black wall sixty feet in front of me with something moving quickly through its base and then the wall closed again and I fired the Deane-Adams. Blue and orange flame splintered the darkness. The report slammed the walls and shook dirt loose from the rafters above.

It deafened me so that the answering shots plopped dully, muzzle flashes like sheets of lightning in that huge black room. Lead sang through the space where I had been standing and chewed through the siding, but I had thrown myself sideways and down immediately after pressing the trigger and it missed me by four feet. I got behind an empty stall. Horses whistled shrilly and kicked at the boards.

"Is that Page Murdock?"

Jordan's call hung in the powder-stinking air. I couldn't place its source. I said it was.

He chuckled. "I did not figure you for as old a trick as that. Were there light in here you would see that my hat is off to you."

The voice seemed to be coming from behind one of the posts that held up the roof. I aimed a little left of the dull creosote gleam and squeezed one off. In the next instant, bullets from two other places struck my stall. I fired at the flashes and hurled myself across the aisle behind the stall opposite. This one had a horse in it, rearing and stamping. I had a sharp pain above my right elbow and reached across with my left hand and drew a splinter six inches long out of the flesh. Blood spouted. I undid my kerchief and tied it one-handed around the upper arm and set the knot with my teeth. I reloaded the five-shot by feel.

"Josh, you hit?" called Jordan.

"No."

"Jer?"

"Nicked m-my hand."

"Bad?"

"Not b-bad."

"G-good," I said.

Jericho cursed and shot. He hadn't moved from his last position and I returned fire.

"Jer?" Jordan called.

No answer. He tried again. Only the horses made any reply. One of the stalls was beginning to go with a crackling noise.

"Jericho was the baby of the family, Murdock," said Jordan after a long silence. "I promised our mother when we left home I would look after him."

"You did a lousy job," I said.

"You should have considered my offer. Any fool can shoot and sit a saddle. It requires a special breed to become rich on top of that. When I came in here I was thinking of asking you in again. But Jericho has changed all that."

I listened to the sounds in the stable. He was talking to cover something.

"How did you make out with those stranglers?" he asked.

I said, "They're dead. All but one. Not counting your brother Joshua."

"No Mercy ever lynched a man."

"A town or a man, what's the difference to a strangler?" I was listening hard now. Under the horses' terrified whinnying and snorting and kicking, wood groaned, slowly, heavily, as under stealthy footsteps.

"We have done no crime," said Jordan Mercy.

"The Judge says different."

"What do you know about the Judge?"

"I talked to him tonight. Your boy Willard didn't want me to but I reasoned with him."

There was a pause.

"You're good, Murdock. But then I always knew that."

"I figure you for arson, too, and assault. You shouldn't have beat up the girl, Mercy. I wouldn't have thought it of you."

"I gave Josh hell about that. He did it on his own."

The spent powder stung my eyes. I rubbed them clear. My right arm throbbed and I could barely feel the gun in that hand. I loosened the tourniquet a notch to let some circulation into my fingers. While I was doing that a handful of dirt sifted down in front of my face from the loft overhead.

I stood up fast and stepped into the aisle and fired three times almost straight up. After a beat someone went "huh" and wood splintered and a rotted two-by-four tumbled down from the loft and bounced when it hit the earth and an instant later something the size of a bale of hay thudded down on top of it and didn't bounce.

"Josh?"

"No," I said. "Just the crate he came in."

A stall gave away then with a splitting sound and a big white, ghostly in the gloom, vaulted over the debris into the aisle, plunging and bucking and battering the doors with its forefeet. They weren't latched and flew open, spilling light in from the streetlamp outside as the horse galloped for freedom. I got a glimpse of Jordan Mercy standing now with his back to the opening and his coattails spread, crouched with his Smith & Wesson in his right hand, and then he fanned off four rounds so fast they sounded like one long report, flame sputtering from the muzzle. Something burned my left side as I went over fast, snapping off a shot as I did so that hit high up on the wall. Then there was a nasty loud splattering noise and a flash of dazzling red and blue fire that traced a perfect circle like a Lucifer's-wheel in the doorway behind Mercy and he executed a jerking half-pirouette, throwing his gun arm high over his head, and landed on his face.

"My oh my," said Duncan, still wearing my hat and jacket and holding his pepperbox pistol in the smoky square of light. "Ain't Old Sally hard to hang to on to when she does that, though?"

TWENTY-TWO

If you should ever find yourself leafing through the brown and crumbling medical journals of that time, you may come across a paper presented by Robert S. Chrichton, M.D., detailing the long treatment and recovery of one Jordan Abraham Mercy from multiple bullet wounds suffered in the spring of 1880. One of the balls from Duncan's pepperbox had passed through the fleshy part of the marshal's upper arm and another had lodged in the web of muscle and ligaments high on his back, but he had caught the rest low around his vital organs and there was never any reason to suspect he would live. Some Eastern papers carried his obituary, with the result that when he *did* die of pneumonia and complications following the removal of his appendix in 1912, most who heard of it were surprised and thought there had been some mistake. They couldn't have known the mistake was thirty-two years old.

Chrichton took out one kidney and plucked lead splinters out of Mercy's lungs and worried about the liver and closed up and then had to go back in later to sew up a hole he'd missed the first time. He and his wife saw their patient through the long fever of infection and delirium while his brothers were shipped in boxes back to their mother's home in Illinois and Frank Willard was lowered into an unmarked hole in the Helena cemetery. Three months later, thin and pale and prematurely gray, Mercy engaged Devereaux as his attorney and won a change of venue to Wyoming, where he stood up in a Cheyenne court to receive a sentence of fourteen years' hard labor at the federal penitentiary for the crimes of extortion and obstruction of justice. The charges of arson and unlawful imprisonment were dropped by agreement with the prosecution for the sake of expediency and no evidence existed to link Jordan with his brother Joshua's assault on Jackie at Chicago Joe's.

The bullet crease on my left side didn't give Mrs. Chrichton as much trouble as my right arm where the splinter had gone in, piercing an artery and severing some nerves that left my fingertips numb for months afterward. But I was out of her husband's office by morning with my arm in a sling and visiting Jackie in her upstairs bedroom at Joe's. Chrichton had set her broken nose, but she was missing her front teeth and her jaw was swollen and she had two black eyes. I stood holding my hat in the doorway, which was as far as Joe would let me come, and said I was sorry. She didn't answer.

"Can't she talk?" I whispered to Joe.

"She can talk." The madam was tall and calm, with discreet powder in the cracks at the corners of her eyes and her dress buttoned to the neck. "The first time a man hurts you, you take it hard."

I was looking at the bruised face above the bedcovers with bandages on her nose and her yellow hair taken down. She looked even younger than usual. "Anything I can do?"

"You can stay away from her. I can't make you. This business would be in a sorry state if we started picking and choosing the customers. But Jackie hasn't been hurt enough yet to look at the world men like you carry with you."

I said good-bye to Jackie and Joe and got away from there. You don't get much lower than being not good enough for a working girl. I looked in at the livery stable. Duncan grinned at me over the back of the Arabian he was currying. He looked as tired as I felt.

"How's the arm, Mr. Murdock?"

"Sore as hell. Me too. I thought I told you to ditch that iron and keep riding."

"I done tried. Old Sally just kind of stuck to my hand, and I reckon that mare of yours don't like niggers, on account of she turned right around and taken me back into the thick of it."

"I see your boss didn't fire you for shooting up his stable."

"I was all night running down that there horse that got loose in the fracas, else he would of. One of the others pulled up lame from kicking the stall, but the only thing bad hurt here last night was men."

I didn't go into that. Listening to one of Mrs. Chrichton's lectures on guns and killing had been part of the price of getting patched up. "It won't be easy living here," I told Duncan. "Folks get nervous when a black man takes it into his head to start shooting up whites."

"I didn't shoot up but one, and him a crook."

"That won't be the way they'll look at it." I got my star out of my pocket with my good hand and held it out. He didn't take it.

"I reckon I'm used to rocks in the road," he said.

I put the badge away and we shook hands. His grip was as strong as an iron clamp and slippery with liniment.

Judge Blackthorne was just walking in to work when I hit the street in front of the courthouse. Today he had on a tailcoat with a pinched waist and stacked lapels. "I'll

want a detailed report on last night's activities," he said
without greeting. "By noon."

"Yes, sir."

"And see the clerk. You're paying for Willard's burial.
His body's at the undertaker's now."

"You're welcome," I said. But I was speaking to the
courthouse door.

Sugar Jim Creel hanged on schedule for the murder of
the government surveyor. About a thousand people showed
up for the event, packing into the square behind the courthouse with its tall gallows and concessionists working their
way through the crowd selling cold beer and fried chicken
with the drumsticks wearing lace pants. The deputies Mercy
had sent out were back by then and keeping the gathering
orderly with shotguns. Bill Gordon was there, sitting in a
buggy with his bandaged foot propped up on the whip-
socket, presiding over the execution as required by his office as marshal. Sugar Jim mounted to the scaffold in a
clean shirt and pants with his hair pomaded into a showy
pompadour and his hands manacled. Asked if he had any
last words, he looked the gray-faced former preacher who
acted as executioner in the eye and said, "I wish it was
you instead of me." The crowd applauded and cheered.
Sugar Jim was grinning when the black hood came down
over his face. The noose came next and the executioner
snugged the big knot up under Sugar Jim's left ear and
tripped the lever. Sugar Jim kicked just once. When it was
over, the curtains in the window of Judge Blackthorne's
chambers slid shut.

Colonel Aaron Hookstratton was there for the hanging
and wrote it up for the Omaha *Herald* under his Jack Rimfire by-line.

That afternoon I walked out of the Belmont where they
were repairing the fire damage and found the Colonel ele-

vating his substantial rear end onto the driver's seat of his wagon. He was wearing his loud buckskin and the tall black hat that made him look like a fat itinerant Sunday school teacher. Chief Knife-in-the-Belly sat on his pinto in the same dusty shapeless clothes everyone wore for riding and an old Stetson with a hole cut in the crown so his head could breathe. But for his graying braids there was nothing to distinguish him from any other old man. Caesar the buffalo hung his head at the rear of the wagon with flies swaying over his rump.

"Heading out?" I asked Hookstratton.

"There is a range war brewing in Idaho and little enough to rival it here," he said glumly. "Unless, of course, you would care to reconsider my proposition. I am short one gunman."

I shook my head. "Willard called it. He got to reading your dime novels and thought that fast-draw stuff was the way it's done. You see men out here who think that, but you have to look quick. Where's his horse?"

"I sold it. Caesar will have no other beasts walking behind the wagon."

"I guess I'll be reading about the livery stable shoot-out before long."

"No, lawmen shooting at other lawmen just confuses readers back East. And they will not stand to have their heroes bettered by black men. No, my plans remain unchanged. Somewhere there is a man proficient with firearms who will have no objection to the role of hero. I hold faith that we shall find each other."

"So do I," I said. "You'll pardon me if I don't wish you luck."

"You have my pardon, sir. And my sympathy. It is a poor thing not to outlive oneself."

He untied the team's reins and gave them a flip and the

wagon lurched and began rolling. Belly kneed the pinto into motion. I watched them until they made the turn at the end of Main Street and put a building between us, the tall square box rocking from side to side with its gilt lettering ablaze in the sun.

I never saw any of them again, except Duncan and of course Judge Blackthorne and Marshal Gordon, who retired a year later still in great pain from the gout and was replaced by another paper-shuffler who had never had anything to do with law enforcement and owed his presidential appointment to his work on James A. Garfield's campaign. By then Duncan had left his job at the livery stable and gone elsewhere to seek work. "I got no friends here," he told me, stuffing his other shirt and pants and a small stack of books into a gunnysack in his little lean-to room off the stable. I said he was mistaken. Things had gotten hard for him after the Mercy story made the rounds but he wouldn't let me try to do anything about it. I don't know what became of him after he left Helena.

Once when a train robber's trail took me near Painted Rock I stopped in to see the kid, but his stepmother told me he was out stringing fence along the east line. Barbed wire was just starting to come in then on the same wind that carried death to the open range. I asked about his father and learned that the old man had died of a series of strokes only a few months after his son's return from Teamstrike. That was my last visit to the area before most of the ranches were sold and broken up into farms. None of the hard-scrabblers I spoke to then had ever heard of the kid.

When I next saw Great Falls it was during the copper boom. The place had a new sheriff who didn't know anything about the old one and if the old one was still there he was lost in the crowd.

Colonel Aaron Hookstratton and Chief Knife-in-the-

Belly and their buffalo Caesar dropped through a hole someplace.

Not long after Teamstrike I got a letter from Cocker Flynn's sister Sharon in St. Louis, who had read of her brother's death in the papers and wanted details. I wrote back that he had died holding off the stranglers while the kid and I made our escape. I enclosed a bank draft in the amount of the posse pay he had coming and didn't hear from her after that. No reward was ever paid for the Indian or Harvey Byrd or the stranglers.

Jordan Mercy was paroled on good behavior in 1888. Until his death twenty-four years later the one piece of information I picked up on him had him working in a tiny Wild West show attached to a circus touring the southeastern United States. They paid him to plug peach tins on the fly for audiences that had never heard of the Mankiller of Topeka.

Loren D. Estleman is a prolific and versatile author who, since the publication of his first novel in 1976, has established himself as a leading writer of both mystery and Western fiction. His *Aces and Eights* won the 1982 Western Writers of America Golden Spur Award for Best Historical Western, and *This Old Bill* has been nominated for a Pulitzer Prize. He is also the author of the Amos Walker mystery series. Estleman lives in Whitmore Lake, Michigan.